“Return to the s

me.”

Ellie’s heart skipped a
you mean? Do you kno ... asking of
me?”

“It’s been fifteen years. Don’t you think it’s time you went back?”

“I’ve been back.”

“When?”

“A few years ago. I got as far as the doorway.”

“You didn’t go inside?”

“I couldn’t.” A panic attack had frozen her at the doorway. When the paralysis finally subsided, she’d turned and headed for home as fast as she could run and hadn’t dared go back.

“I think you should try again,” Sam said.

“Easy for you to say.”

His voice softened. “There’s nothing to be afraid of. I’ll be with you every step of the way.”

That note in his voice...the way he looked at her...

She had *everything* to be afraid of.

SOMEONE IS WATCHING

AMANDA STEVENS

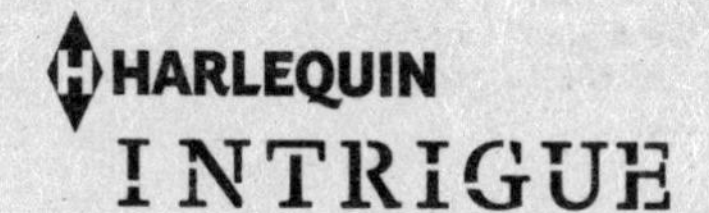

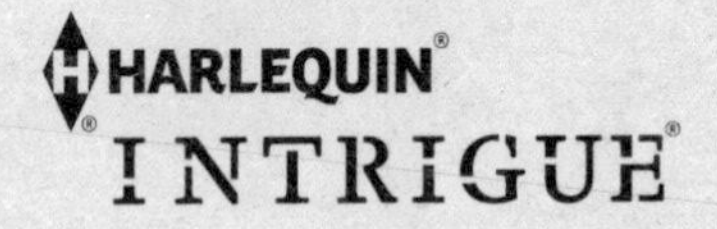

ISBN-13: 978-1-335-13665-7

Recycling programs for this product may not exist in your area.

Someone Is Watching

This edition published by arrangement with Harlequin Books S.A.

For questions and comments about the quality of this book, please contact us at CustomerService@Harlequin.com.

Harlequin Enterprises ULC
22 Adelaide St. West, 40th Floor
Toronto, Ontario M5H 4E3, Canada
www.Harlequin.com

Printed in U.S.A.

Amanda Stevens is an award-winning author of over fifty novels, including the modern gothic series The Graveyard Queen. Her books have been described as eerie and atmospheric, and "a new take on the classic ghost story." Born and raised in the rural South, she now resides in Houston, Texas, where she enjoys binge-watching, bike riding and the occasional margarita.

Books by Amanda Stevens

Harlequin Intrigue

An Echo Lake Novel

Without a Trace
A Desperate Search
Someone Is Watching

Twilight's Children

Criminal Behavior
Incriminating Evidence
Killer Investigation

Pine Lake
Whispering Springs

Bishop's Rock (ebook novella)

MIRA Books

The Graveyard Queen

The Restorer
The Kingdom
The Prophet
The Visitor
The Sinner
The Awakening

Visit the Author Profile page at Harlequin.com.

CAST OF CHARACTERS

Ellie Brannon—The host of a late-night talk radio show receives phone calls from a frightened woman claiming to be her best friend who went missing fifteen years ago.

Special Agent Sam Reece—The Riley Cavanaugh kidnapping was his first big case. He's haunted by the possibility that his arrogance and inexperience allowed Riley Cavanaugh's abductor to go free.

Jenna Malloy—She and Riley went missing from the Ruins on the night of a blood moon. She was found three weeks later, but the key to what really happened that night remains deeply buried in her subconscious.

Hazel Lamont—Jenna's enigmatic new roommate may exert a dangerous influence over the troubled woman.

Madeline Keyes—The ruthless and ambitious reporter is certain Ellie Brannon knows more than she's telling about Riley's disappearance.

Cory Small—His uncle disappeared on the same night the girls went missing. Did he and his mother help Silas Creed escape?

Silas Creed aka Preacher—A former psychiatric patient, he remains the main suspect in the kidnapping. Fifteen years after Riley and Jenna were taken, has he come back for Ellie Brannon—the girl who got away?

Chapter One

For the past three nights, Ellie Brannon had been receiving staticky messages from an unknown caller on the open-line portion of her radio program. The reception was so poor she could barely make out the anonymous caller's voice, let alone the broken message. But there was something disturbing about the timing of the calls. Something unsettling about the frenetic undertone that sputtered through the white noise.

Cocooned as she was in her soundproof studio, Ellie could normally lose herself to the weird and unusual stories brought to her via her most avid listeners.

The subject matter she covered ran the gamut from paranormal activity to political conspiracies to unsolved mysteries. Unlike most talk radio hosts, Ellie refused to use a screener despite the fact that *Midnight on Echo Lake* was now broadcast on sixty stations around the country, as well as live-streamed on the popular internet radio network where she'd gotten her first big break.

Adjusting the microphone arm, she glanced at the clock on the wall, noting the time as she pushed the blinking button and greeted the caller.

Static once again crackled in her headphones.

"Go ahead, Caller. You're on the air with Ellie Brannon."

The reception cleared for a moment, allowing the woman's urgent whisper to come through loud and clear. "He's coming..."

Ellie ignored the shivers down her back as she kept her tone even. "I'm getting a lot of noise in my ear, Caller. Can you move the phone away from the radio?"

The voice faded as the interference rose to a deafening crescendo. Ellie fiddled with the slider on the audio console as she tried to filter out the annoying clatter. "Caller, are you still there?"

Nothing now but chilling silence.

Ellie's hands trembled as she adjusted the controls. She didn't know why. Strange calls were her raison d'être, but something about the persistence of this particular caller unnerved her.

Probably a prankster.

Ellie was accustomed to a fair amount of prank calls, though not as many as one might expect given the premise of her show. Most people who took the time to call in just wanted a chance to tell their story in a forum that didn't openly ridicule or pass judgment. But from time to time, some of the local teenagers dared each other to call in with outlandish stories about alien abductions just as they'd once goaded their classmates to spend the night in the Ruins, an abandoned psychiatric hospital not far from Ellie's studio. On a clear night, she could see the smokestack rising up through the pine trees as she trekked the short distance from her studio to her back deck. Sometimes, if she was feeling brave, she would walk down to the dock and sit with her feet dangling in the water as she traced the crumbling roofline and remembered.

On most nights, though, she hurried inside her house and locked the doors. Still. After all these years.

He's coming...

With a start, she realized she'd broken the golden rule of radio—no dead air. Shrugging off the final caller, she queued up the closing music. "You've been listening to open-line Wednesday on the After Dark Network. I'm your host, Ellie Brannon, signing off from the banks of eerie Echo Lake..."

Wrapping up her callout, she turned off the mic and removed her headphones as the on-air lights winked off on her console and over the studio door.

What now?

She tried reversing the call using star-sixty-nine but nothing went through. Should she contact her brother? Tom was the Nance County sheriff. If someone was in trouble, he needed to know. But the call could have come from any part of the country. Or even out of the country. It was probably nothing more than a prank call, anyway. If someone were really in trouble, why not notify the authorities instead of calling in every night to a syndicated radio show?

Go home. Have a glass of wine, listen to some music and relax. Maybe take a long bath to unwind.

Sound advice, yet she lingered, checking the log to match the time the call had come in to the previous two nights. A screener would have required a name and location before putting the call through to Ellie, but she had nothing more to go on than *Unknown Caller.*

Locking everything down for the night, she left the studio and hurried along the path to her house. The moon hung low over the lake, silvering the water and casting long shadows along the bank. The eerie wail of a loon sent another tingle down her spine. At least it wasn't the scream of a peacock, though she was used to that screech by now. Her nearest neighbor had died some time back, leaving Ellie to care for the peafowl that roosted on her property.

She was only a few feet away from her back steps when the wail segued into a tremolo, the maniacal laughing sound of a loon sensing danger. Ellie turned to sweep the water. The surface was calm and the air still, but she imagined she could hear the low grumble of an outboard motor somewhere in the distance. The bullfrogs and crickets had long since gone silent. The predators owned the night.

What a creepy thought.

She'd allowed herself to get caught up in the spookiness of her surroundings and those staticky phone calls and now she felt the *thump, thump, thump* of an accelerated heartbeat, the cold sweat and tightened chest of paralyzing fear. She hadn't suffered a panic attack in years, but she recognized the signs. The old defensive exercises came back to her automatically. *Take deep breaths. Find a focal point. Picture your happy place.*

The techniques worked if she allowed them to, but her instinct at the moment was to rush headlong for the house. She knew better. A full-blown episode could debilitate her for hours. Or she might stumble and fall on the uneven terrain in her freak-out. Better that she take the time to ward off that dark visitor.

Drawing in slow measured breaths, she found a distant spot on the lake where moonlight gleamed down through the cypress branches, creating delicate twinkles on the surface, like the dance of a thousand fairies. Ellie pictured herself in a boat, trailing her fingers through that cool shimmering water. Drifting, just drifting…

After a few moments, her heartbeat slowed and she turned back to the path, forcing herself to take her time. There was nothing to be afraid of in the woods. How long had she lived out here alone? Five years? Or was it six now? Despite the recent spike in violent crime in Nance County, she'd been perfectly safe in her bungalow. Nothing truly scary had happened to her since—

A twig snapped behind her and she whirled, peering into the woods even as she chided herself for an overactive imagination. Had a few prank calls really put her this much on edge?

He's coming...

Thump, thump, thump went her heart.

Focus on the shimmers...

Taking another deep breath, she turned back to the house, using the solar lights that lined the pathway to guide her to the deck steps. She went up quickly and didn't linger outside to enjoy the night air. Letting herself in the back door, she turned the deadbolt and quickly reached for the light switch, leaning against the wall in relief as illumination flooded her tidy kitchen. She concentrated on her breathing for several more minutes until the tightness in her chest eased and she felt steady on her feet.

Opening a bottle of wine, she took a glass with her upstairs where she settled for a hot shower rather than a long bath. Shrugging into her favorite robe, she went back downstairs to replenish her drink, carrying both stemware and bottle into her cozy den where she curled up on the sectional to watch late-night TV.

She dozed. Sometime later a loud noise awakened her. She thought she was dreaming at first. Even lying with her eyes wide open, she wasn't certain the banging on her front door was real.

Her movements were sluggish as she sat up and glanced around the room, eerily illuminated by the flickering TV. She switched off the flat screen with the remote, wondering if the sound had come from the infomercial that had taken over the airwaves since she fell asleep. Reaching for her phone, she checked the time. Then she got up, still lethargic, still mostly unconcerned until the doorbell rang in quick staccato bursts that startled her fully awake.

She bolted upright on a gasp, realizing that the pounding on her door, the flickering TV and the infomercial had all been incorporated into her dream.

She wasn't dreaming now.

Rising for real this time, she pulled her robe around her as she moved to the front window to glance out. The moon was still up, unnaturally brilliant as its light glowed over the pine forest. She could see all the way down her driveway to the main road. No parked cars. No lurking shadows. She checked the back door, letting her gaze move across the deck and slowly down the steps to the dock. Despite the full moon, the shadows were deep along the bank. A mild breeze stirred the Spanish moss that hung in heavy layers at the water's edge.

Retracing her steps through the house, Ellie removed a key from a carved box on the console table in the foyer. She held it in her palm for a moment before unlocking the drawer and removing the small pistol she kept there for protection. She had another like it in her nightstand drawer upstairs.

Her late father had been the Nance County sheriff for nearly thirty years. He'd made certain that she and her brother knew how to respect and handle weapons from an early age, and after the disappearances, he'd insisted that Ellie learn how to protect herself.

If she'd settled down in a more populated area, she doubted she would have wanted a gun in the house. Living alone on Echo Lake was a different matter. Out here, she was miles from town, miles from help. A stone's throw from the place where her friends had been taken and where she'd been left for dead. Her location was by design, of course. The result of a promise she'd long ago made to herself. *Stare down the monster or you'll never be free of him.*

Keeping the pistol at her side, she peered through the sidelight. The motion detector flood on her front porch had come on. She had a clear view of the steps and the yard. No one was out there now, but the light had recently been activated. Raccoons, possums and stray cats were the usual culprits, but an animal hadn't rung her doorbell.

Another prank? A harmless game of Ring and Run?

It wouldn't be the first time. The subject matter of her radio program invited mockery. Some of the local teenagers had started hanging out at the Ruins again. She'd seen the bobble of their flashlights along the bank lately, had heard the whoops of their laughter as she sat out on the dock. She tried not to think harshly of their mischief. She'd been a teenager once, susceptible to peer pressure and the tug of her own curiosity.

There'd been a blood moon on the night she and her friends had ventured into the Ruins, but she wouldn't think about that right now. She wouldn't dwell on the creaking floorboards that should have been a warning or the gleam of eyes that had watched from the shadows. She wouldn't dwell on the lost memories of that night, the survivor's guilt that still dogged her after all these years or the violent images that came to her in dreams from time to time.

She wouldn't dwell on any of that, even though all of it had brought her back to Echo Lake.

She kept watch at the window for the longest time. Nothing seemed amiss. Whoever had been at her front door was either long gone or watched from the bushes to see how she reacted. Maybe if she went outside and waved her gun about, they'd turn tail and run. Might think twice about their next little game of Ring and Run.

Of course, she would never behave in such a reckless

manner. She would never knowingly terrorize anyone over a silly prank.

Locking the gun back in the drawer, she returned the key to the box and told herself to turn in. Forget about pranks. Forget about those disturbing calls. *Just get some rest. Everything will be fine in the morning.*

The good news was, she'd managed to fend off a panic attack and she could take comfort in knowing she was stronger for it.

Even so, sleep was a long time coming. When she finally dozed off, images of a demonic face flickered across her subconscious like the strobe of an unwatched TV.

SAM REECE COULDN'T sleep. He sat out on the balcony of his Dallas townhome and watched the shimmer of moonlight on the surface of the landscaped pond that curved around the gated community. The streets were empty at this hour, the neighborhood almost preternaturally silent. Earlier, he'd spotted a young couple out walking their dog, but they'd long since scurried home.

An odd restiveness plagued him, though he had no idea why. He liked it here well enough, having settled in a quaint area of town halfway between the hustle and bustle of downtown and One Justice Way where he worked. Maybe the neighborhood was a little too laid-back at times, but at thirty-seven, he no longer felt the need to be in the mix. The proximity of bars and restaurants had become less important to him than quiet neighbors.

There'd been a time not so long ago when he never

would have imagined himself in such a place. Never would have considered a voluntary reassignment to any field office—let alone Dallas—after spending so many years in DC. Maybe he was going through some sort of pre-midlife crisis, feeling the pull of his roots more strongly than the soar of his wings. He'd grown up in northeast Texas and had cut his teeth in the Tyler satellite office after Quantico. Eventually, he'd been transferred to the Dallas field office and from there to FBI headquarters where he'd spent the past ten years as a member and then leader of one of the first Child Abduction Rapid Deployment teams in the country.

It had been an exciting, fast-paced life, grueling in some ways, but Sam had always thrived on chaos and clutter. He lived for new challenges and liked nothing more than the exhilaration of a complicated case. Yet here he was back on his old stomping grounds.

He reminded himself that Dallas was hardly a demotion. The field office was one of the busiest in the country with no shortage of stimulating cases. But in all honesty, he hadn't come back because of boredom or even to be close to his family. He'd come back because his first case still haunted him.

On the night of a blood moon, three teenagers in Belle Pointe, Texas, had entered the ruins of an abandoned psychiatric hospital. One of the girls had been found unconscious the next morning at the edge of the lake. Another girl had been spotted a few weeks later wandering along the side of a country road in a fugue state. The third girl, Riley Cavanaugh, had never been seen or heard from again.

In the days and weeks following her disappearance, the local authorities had combed the countryside and interviewed dozens if not hundreds of witnesses. In desperation, they'd finally requested help from the Bureau. Sam, fresh out of Quantico with a savior complex the size of Texas, had been sent in to offer assistance. He'd used all the federal resources at his disposal, but Riley Cavanaugh had never been found and her kidnapper remained elusive to this day.

Sam had done everything by the book. Everything in his power to find and bring that girl home. He had no regrets as to his conduct, but if he'd had more experience or a deeper insight into the criminal mind, things might have worked out differently.

The two survivors—Ellie Brannon and Jenna Malloy—hadn't been forthcoming. Jenna had been deeply traumatized by her captivity. Her reticence was understandable. Ellie Brannon was another story. Sam had suspected all along that she was hiding something, maybe even from herself. To this day, he wondered if the key to solving Riley Cavanaugh's disappearance was still tucked away somewhere in Ellie Brannon's subconscious.

Which was why, for the past few years, he'd been tuning in to her radio show every chance he got. *Midnight on Echo Lake.* An evocative name for a strange broadcast patterned, he supposed, after the more famous *Coast to Coast AM.* At first he'd listened to try to pick up on subtle clues and gain some insight into the host. Ellie's calm demeanor and soothing voice kept him coming back. He wondered what she was like these days in real life. She'd been a frightened kid when he'd last seen her, wary, defensive and perhaps a little intimidated by the presence of an FBI agent, even one still wet behind the ears.

Jenna Malloy had been the opposite. She'd taken to Sam when she'd refused to see anyone else, including her family and, for a time, Ellie Brannon. After he'd been transferred to DC, he'd still managed to touch base with her now and then. Maybe that had been a mistake. She had a tendency to fixate and he'd been forced to set some boundaries.

Strange how he hadn't heard from her in a couple of years and then all of a sudden in the past few weeks, he'd gotten a spate of phone calls and letters. It was almost as if she'd somehow intuited his return to Dallas before he'd known himself he was coming back.

Now that they were in the same city, he'd have to be careful how he handled their interaction. He didn't want to turn his back on her, but neither could he allow her to think of him as a friend. He needed to maintain professional distance, but that wasn't always easy when he remembered the shape she'd been in after her rescue. She'd spent the first two years after her captivity in one mental health facility after another. Sam could still picture her sitting in front of the large window at the Penn Shepherd Hospital in Dallas staring absentmindedly out at the grounds until she would turn, blue eyes shimmering with quiet excitement as the fog lifted and she recognized his features.

Special Agent Reece! How nice of you to come and see me.

How are you feeling today, Jenna?

Better, I think.

That's good to hear.

Can I ask a favor of you, Agent Reece?

Of course. What is it?

I would like it very much if you called me Jenny, the way Riley used to.

All right...Jenny.

You have no idea how happy that makes me. Will you say it again?

Let's focus on something else, shall we? I'd like to ask you some questions if that's okay.

I guess so. But I hope you haven't come to talk about her *again.*

You mean Riley?

You know that's not who I mean.

Why don't you want to talk about Ellie Brannon?

She left me there. She left us both. We were her best friends. Like sisters, she used to call us. I don't understand how she could have done such a thing.

I don't think she had a choice. She was found unconscious at the edge of the lake the next morning. If her brother hadn't acted as quickly as he had, she would have died.

There are worse things than dying, Agent Reece.

I'm well aware, Jenny.

The ringtone on Sam's cell phone crashed the memory. He checked the screen, startled to see Jenna's name on the caller ID. How could she possibly have known he was sitting out here in the dark, thinking about her? Sometimes her intuition seemed downright uncanny.

He considered letting the call go to voice mail, but his conscience wouldn't let him. "Hello, Jenna."

"It's Jenny, remember?" She sounded peeved.

He kept his voice moderate but firm. "Do you have any idea what time it is?"

"I know it's late, but you're still up, aren't you?"

He scanned his surroundings, peering between buildings and down each street. Was she out there somewhere watching him? He didn't think that likely and yet he felt an inexplicable apprehension. "You couldn't have known that, though. We agreed you would only call during the workday at a preset time, remember?"

"This couldn't wait."

"Even until morning?"

She sighed. "You're angry with me."

"I'm not angry. I just want to make sure you understand our agreement."

"Of course I understand. I'm not a child. But sometimes there are extenuating circumstances."

"What are the circumstances?"

She didn't say anything for the longest moment.

"Jenny? Are you still there?"

"Yes, I'm here."

He searched the darkness. "Tell me what's on your mind tonight."

"A lot of things, actually. Did you know that I have a new job?"

He tried to temper his impatience. "That's great, but you didn't call me at one o'clock in the morning to talk about a new job, did you?"

"I also have a new place. I'm not far from you now."

He rubbed the back of his neck where the hair at his nape suddenly stood on end. "How do you know where I live?"

Another long silence.

Sam got up and paced to the end of the balcony. The moon was up and the grounds were well lit, but the shadows on the other side of the pond were impenetrable. He told himself that even if she'd somehow managed to ferret out his address, she wouldn't be able to get through the gate without a code. But as he knew only too well, there were ways of breaching any space if one wanted in badly enough. Jenna Malloy was nothing if not resourceful.

"Don't worry, Agent Reece. The location is just a coincidence."

Was it?

"My roommate had already rented the house when she invited me to move in with her. Her name is Hazel. Don't you love that name? So dreamy and old-fashioned, although there's nothing traditional about Hazel Lamont. She's unlike anyone I've ever known."

Sam wasn't in the mood for chitchat, but he also knew better than to allow annoyance to creep into his voice. His relationship with Jenna Malloy was unorthodox and not without risk, but he always had the hope that something would come back to her during one of their conversations. That something would still break in the Riley Cavanaugh case.

"How did the two of you meet?" he asked.

"Oh, we've known each other for quite some time. I

guess you could say we met through a mutual acquaintance. We have a lot in common."

"That's great. I'm happy for you," Sam said. "But you also didn't call to talk to me about your new roommate."

"No, I didn't. I'm just making small talk to try to calm my nerves. It's an exercise one of my therapists taught me a long time ago."

"Why are you nervous?"

Her voice lowered to a near whisper. "I'm not just nervous. I'm scared, Agent Reece."

Suddenly she sounded young and vulnerable, and Sam remembered why he always tried to hold back his irritation even when she crossed an uncomfortable line. He'd never been able to shake the image of her on that lonely country road, eyes haunted as she clutched a dirty blanket around her frail shoulders. He'd never been able to forget the photographs and medical reports that had graphically documented her abuse.

"What are you afraid of?" he asked gently.

"Weren't you listening tonight?"

He knew what she meant, but he asked anyway. "You mean to Ellie Brannon's radio program? I missed it tonight. I didn't get home until late."

"She called again, Agent Reece."

"Who called?"

"Riley."

"You know that's not possible."

Jenna's voice rose in agitation. "I don't know anything of the sort and neither do you. Her body was never found. She could still be alive for all we know."

"That's highly unlikely after all this time."

"Well, *someone* has been calling into Ellie's show for the past three nights. She's been calling me, too, Agent Reece."

"What?" Sam leaned against the railing as he tried to quell his unease. The night was still quiet. The brick wall that surrounded the community muted the traffic noises, and yet the darkness suddenly seemed alive with prying eyes and creeping shadows. His imagination, of course. No one was about this time of night. Not here. Not inside his protected haven. Outside the gates, where Jenna Malloy dwelled, was another matter.

"Why are you only mentioning this now?" he asked.

"Because I wanted to make sure it was Riley. She always calls at night. Maybe that's the only time she can get away. Sometimes the phone goes dead as soon as I answer, but sometimes I can hear her breathing."

"How do you know it's Riley?"

"She started to cry once. Tiny little sobs that reminded me of a lost kitten. It made me cry, too, Agent Reece. I felt so helpless, not knowing where she was or how I could help her."

"Have you told anyone else about these calls?"

"Like my therapist, you mean? She wouldn't believe me."

He chose his words carefully. "The caller says nothing, but you're convinced she's Riley?"

"Yes."

"How long has this been going on?"

"A few days, I guess. You know how I sometimes lose track of time."

"What did she say tonight when she called the radio show?"

"She said he's coming."

"That's it?"

"Isn't that enough, Agent Reece? What more would you want her to say?"

"This isn't the first time you've heard Riley's voice," he reminded her. "You were once convinced she was living down the street from you. You said you spotted her at the bus stop, remember?"

"This is different," she insisted. "I was confused in the past. I know that now. I sometimes couldn't tell the difference between fantasy and reality. I blame that on all the medication they were giving me in that awful place. But I'm better now." Her voice dropped again. "She doesn't just call, Agent Reece. She was at my house tonight. That's why I *had* to call you. I didn't think I should wait until morning to tell you."

"You saw her?"

"No, but she left something on my front porch. A gift that has meaning only to me."

"Can you be more specific?"

"Since we were little girls, Riley and I both loved peacocks. It was our thing. A local woman used to raise them and we would ride our bikes out to the lake to watch them. Sometimes we'd find their feathers on the ground and Riley collected them. She left a peacock feather on my front porch as a message. She's trying to let me know that she's alive and in trouble."

"If that were the case, why wouldn't she go to the police?" Sam reasoned. "Why take the time to leave a feather on your porch, much less to call in to Ellie Brannon's radio show?"

Jenna once again fell silent. When she finally spoke, her voice was still low but surprisingly determined despite an underlying tremor. "I was held against my will for nearly three weeks. Nineteen days of unspeakable horror. When I was found wandering down the side of that road, I had no idea where I was or where I'd been. I could barely speak. I didn't know enough to flag down a car for help, let alone call the police. Riley has been with that monster for fifteen years. *Fifteen years*, Agent Reece. Can you even imagine such a thing? Can we really expect her to behave in a rational manner? She's found a window and she's reaching out in the only way she knows how."

Her argument was so compelling that Sam found himself buying into the possibility before he mentally shook himself. Riley Cavanaugh had disappeared without a trace fifteen years ago. The chances she could still be alive were miniscule. Hallucinations or a cruel hoax was the more logical explanation.

But if there was even the slightest chance…

"Maybe we should set a time to meet so we can discuss this further," Sam said.

Jenna said eagerly, "Yes, of course. We have to figure out what to do next, don't we? If she's somehow managed to get away, he'll come for her again. He's probably out there looking for her at this very minute."

Sam tried to reel her back in. "Let's not get ahead of ourselves, okay?"

"But we've wasted too much time as it is!"

"Jenna—"

"Promise me you'll find her. Promise me you won't give up like you did last time."

The accusation stung like the point of a white-hot dagger. "I never gave up," Sam said quietly.

"Then go find her, Agent Reece. Go find her before *he* does."

Chapter Two

Ellie awakened again before dawn. Not from a knock on her front door this time, but from a vivid dream that left her trembling with dread. The funny thing was she couldn't remember much about it, only that she'd been running down a dark corridor, trying to flee a nameless, faceless assailant. Or had she been running from her past?

She got up and reached for the water bottle on her nightstand, carrying it with her to the bedroom window. From her vantage, she could see all the way across the lake where a fishing cabin perched on stilts at the edge of the piney woods. The owner had recently died and now the cabin sat dark and forlorn against a backdrop of feathery bowers.

A few stars twinkled out, dimmed by the light of the approaching dawn. As Ellie stood there, sipping tepid water, she had the strangest sensation of floating in time, of being suspended in a haze of lost memories. Once, she would have tried to piece together the fragments that came back to her now and then, but she'd long ago learned that some things were best left alone.

Her brother used to ask her if she'd moved out to the lake hoping the proximity to the Ruins would prod her memory. Maybe in the beginning, but mostly she hadn't wanted to live in fear for the rest of her life. She hadn't wanted to spend her time worrying about a monster in her closet or a depraved psycho watching from the shadows. If she could live so near to where her best friends had been taken, then she could face anything. She could take on the monster without flinching. Or at least without cowering under the covers in sheer terror.

She'd worked very hard for a very long time to get to this point. In some ways, her fear had been easier to conquer than her guilt, but she'd managed to come to terms with what had happened. She would probably never know why she'd been spared—if one could call being left for dead spared. Maybe because she'd been the sheriff's daughter and the kidnapper had feared a more intense search. Or maybe he'd only wanted two captives and Ellie hadn't fit a certain criteria in looks or personality. She'd learned years ago that it was pointless to speculate about the unknowable. It was better to focus on the things in her life she could control.

Smothering a yawn, she stretched her arms over her head to work out the kinks. She had a long day ahead of her. People had the notion that her job entailed nothing more than showing up in her studio to chat with callers and guests, but being on the air for three hours a night, five days a week required a lot of preparation. Her workday started no later than nine in the morning and ended at midnight when she signed off. Long hours required adequate rest, but she knew she wouldn't be able to get back to sleep. Might as well go down and make coffee.

She started to turn away from the window when a movement at the edge of the lake caught her attention. Ellie's heart thudded even as she told herself it was nothing more than a shadow or a tree limb waving in the breeze. But the longer she stared, the more defined the silhouette became until she was certain the intruder was female.

Ellie couldn't make out her features. She was too far away and the shadows were too deep along the bank. But as she stood there, watching, the woman whirled as if startled by a noise in the woods. Then slowly she turned and lifted her head toward Ellie's window.

Their gazes connected for the longest moment. Ellie could have sworn the woman mouthed something up to her. That had to be her imagination. She couldn't even see the woman's features. Maybe this wasn't real, just another waking dream.

The woman glanced over her shoulder. Then she shot one last glance up at Ellie's window before she plunged deeper into the shadows and disappeared into the woods.

Ellie put her hand on the glass as she leaned in, trying to catch another glance. Clearly, someone was playing a cruel joke on her. Whoever the woman was, she knew Ellie's house well enough to look up at her bedroom window.

The ringtone of her cell phone shattered the loaded silence, leaving Ellie trembling as she moved back to her nightstand to glance at the screen. *Unknown Caller.*

She told herself to let the call go to voice mail. Someone was messing with her big time. Someone wanted her scared and on edge, but why?

She snatched up the phone and lifted it to her ear. "Hello?"

Nothing but static.

"Hello? Hello?"

"He's coming," a whispery voice warned through the crackles.

Ellie's fingers curled around the plastic case. "Who is this?"

Silence.

"What do you want?"

Silence.

Ellie closed her eyes. "Why are you doing this?"

"He's coming, Elle."

She stifled a gasp at the nickname. No one had called her that in a very long time. "Who's coming?"

"Preacher," said the whispery voice.

"Preacher is dead," Ellie said fiercely.

"He's not dead, Elle. He's coming back for you."

Cold sweat beaded across her brow as she clutched the phone. "Even if he were alive, why would he risk coming back here after all this time?"

A wrenching pause. "Because you're the one that got away."

Ellie tracked her brother's flashlight beam as he walked the bank and then disappeared into the woods. He was gone for a good thirty minutes before she heard his footsteps on the deck. She went outside to join him and they sat drinking coffee as the sun climbed over the horizon and the sky turned a flaming pink. Streamers of mist hung like wet cotton from the treetops. The day was already warm and still, the early morning silence broken only by the melodic whistle of an overeager wood thrush.

When Tom had first arrived, Ellie had played him the recording of the call that had come in during the previous night's broadcast and now she reluctantly admitted to her near-panic attack on the way home.

"This has really got you wound up," Tom said as he stretched his long legs in front of him.

"The calls that came in on Monday and Tuesday night were so staticky. I could barely make out a voice. As you heard for yourself, last night was different."

"Last night's call came in at the same time as the others?"

"Yes. They seem timed to be the last call of the show."

"After you signed off, you came straight home?"

"Except for the brief panic attack on the trail. I took a shower, drank some wine and fell asleep on the couch."

"How much wine?"

"Not enough that I hallucinated the doorbell or the woman staring up at my window."

"Did you happen to notice the time when the doorbell woke you up?"

"It was a little after one."

"What did you do after that?"

"I went up to bed, but it took me awhile to fall asleep.

Just before dawn, I woke up again and that's when I saw the woman down by the lake."

"What woke you up?"

"A nightmare, I think."

He frowned. "You're having nightmares again? Why didn't you tell me?"

She tried to shrug off his concern. "Everybody has nightmares now and then. I'm not going to bother you every time I have a bad dream."

He looked as if he wanted to argue, but asked instead, "What happened then?"

"That's when I got the next call." Ellie raked fingers through her tangled hair. "I know how all this sounds, but it wasn't a dream or a hallucination. I'm not making any of this up."

"I never thought you were."

"Obviously, it's someone's idea of a sick joke. I probably shouldn't have bothered you with any of this."

He gave her a stern scrutiny. "You're not bothering me. You know you can always call me about anything. That's what brothers are for."

"You're not just my brother, though. You're also the county sheriff. I don't like wasting your time."

"Listen to me. You call whenever you need me. I'll let you know when and if I think you're wasting my time. Agreed?"

Ellie nodded, wrapping her hands around the warm mug. "You didn't find anything down by the lake?" she asked reluctantly.

"I saw some footprints along the bank. A broken

twig or two at the edge of the woods." He sipped slowly. "When was the last time you walked down that way?"

"Late yesterday afternoon when I went over to the Thayer house to feed the peacocks."

"Some of those prints are probably yours then. Now that it's daylight, we can go down and have a look around together. But I think you're right. Someone is having a go at you. Ever since Sophie's disappearance and all that business with Jackson, Riley's kidnapping has been in the news again," he said, referring to a recent kidnapping incident involving yet another Cavanaugh.

Ellie let her head fall back against the rocker as she stared out over the water. Such a peaceful scene and yet her thoughts were increasingly chaotic. "The caller said Preacher is coming back for me."

"You know that's not possible."

She turned to study her brother's profile. "Do I? For all any of us knows, he's still out there somewhere."

"Silas Creed would be an old man by now. If he isn't dead, he's likely incarcerated for another crime. He's not coming back."

"She called me Elle."

Tom shrugged. "I sometimes call you Elle. That doesn't prove anything."

She gave him a reproachful look. "You rarely call me Elle. Riley was the only one who used that name on a regular basis."

"She's not coming back, either, sis."

"I know. It's just..." She shot him an anxious look. "You believe that I saw someone down there, don't you?

I didn't dream her up. I didn't imagine those phone calls or someone ringing my doorbell."

"You certainly didn't imagine the caller who phoned into your radio program last night. I heard the recording myself," Tom reminded her.

Doubt still niggled, but Ellie hated giving voice to her old worries. She folded her arms defensively as she searched the lake.

"What is it?" Tom coaxed.

"What if that phone call somehow set everything else into motion?"

"What do you mean?"

"It triggered a panic attack. Maybe it also awakened old memories. Old fears. Maybe everything else that came afterward really was a dream. Or maybe I'm losing it," she said. "It wouldn't be the first time."

"A minute ago, you were certain it wasn't a dream."

"Maybe I was trying to convince myself."

He placed his cup on the floor beside his rocker and turned to face her. "It's not surprising you're on edge. Anyone would be rattled. That doesn't mean you're losing it. It just means you're human."

"You're a good brother, Tom. Don't let anyone tell you otherwise."

"I'll remind you of that next time you're on my case." He picked up his cup and turned back to the sunrise.

They sat in companionable silence while they drank their coffee. Ellie could tell that Tom had dressed in a hurry after her call. Later, he'd take more care with his appearance, discarding the sneakers for his signature polished boots. As the Nance County sheriff, he had a certain image to uphold. Ellie had no such restrictions. Shorts, tank top and canvas slip-ons were her everyday summer uniform.

She bent and swatted a mosquito at her ankle. "If you believe the woman I saw by the lake was real, then why don't you have more questions about her?"

"Is there something else I need to know? I assumed you'd told me everything."

"I told you everything I remember, but maybe the right question will jog my memory. Don't be afraid to challenge me. Don't treat me any different than you would anyone else who'd called you out at the crack of dawn."

Tom nodded. "All right, then. You say you didn't get a look at her face, but you saw her silhouette. What about height, weight?"

"She was about my size, but taller, I think."

"What about her hair? Long, short, curly, straight?"

Ellie closed her eyes, summoning an image. "I had the impression she was blond." Like Riley. Like Ellie herself. "I remember the way moonlight gleamed off the strands when she whirled toward the woods."

"What about her clothes?"

"A white dress, I think. Or a nightgown."

"You said she looked up at your window and mouthed something to you. Yet it was too dark to make out her features."

Ellie pounced. "See? I knew you didn't believe me."

"I never said that. If you're asking whether or not I think Riley Cavanaugh called tonight to warn you about Preacher or that she came to your house to stare up at your bedroom window, then the answer is no. I don't believe that. But I do believe someone is messing with you. Probably some bored kids egging each other on, but whoever it is and whatever their motivation, I don't like it. Maybe you should come stay in town for a few days until all this blows over."

"I have to prepare for tonight's show and besides, you and Rae don't need me underfoot while you're trying to plan a wedding."

"She wouldn't mind."

"*I* mind. You two deserve this time together."

Tom and Rae Cavanaugh had gotten engaged at the start of the summer. Funny how things sometimes worked out, Ellie reflected. For most of their adult lives, Rae had blamed Tom for her sister's disappearance. They'd barely spoken to one another in the fifteen years since Riley had gone missing and now here they were planning to spend the rest of their lives together.

Ellie was happy for her brother, but their bliss sometimes served to magnify her loneliness. She would never want Tom to know that, of course. He was still the protective big brother. He didn't need another reason to worry about her.

He gave her a look.

"What?" she asked.

"There's something you need to know. I probably should have brought it up when I first got here."

Ellie straightened. She didn't like his tone. "What is it?"

"Do you remember that reporter named Melanie

Kent? The one that wrote the series of articles about Riley's disappearance?"

Icy fingers curled around the base of Ellie's spine. "I'm not likely to forget her. She made our lives a living hell until you finally exposed her. Why are you bringing her up now?"

Tom paused. "She may be back in town."

Ellie shot forward, clutching the arms of her chair. "What? What do you mean *may* be back in town?"

He could hardly meet her gaze. "I haven't seen her myself, but Rae said one of her cousins at the newspaper told her Melanie had applied for a job there."

"When was this?"

"Recently. In the last week or two."

"And you're just now telling me?" Ellie's voice rose in agitation. "You didn't think this was something I needed to know?"

"She didn't get the job," Tom said. "I'd hoped she'd leave town as quietly as she came in."

"But she didn't."

"I don't know. I haven't been able to locate her."

"Tom." Ellie stared daggers at her brother. "I can't believe you didn't tell me."

He shrugged helplessly. "I knew it would upset you. I was trying to protect you."

"By allowing me to be blindsided by a woman who tried to destroy me?"

"When you put it like that." He winced. "You're right. I should have told you."

Ellie tried to quell her anger as she settled back in her chair. Taking out her frustration on Tom wasn't going to help anything. If Melanie Kent was back in town, they needed to stick together.

Melanie had first entered their lives when Ellie was a junior in college. A few weeks into a new assignment as host for a call-in show at the university radio station, Ellie had started receiving calls from a troubled young woman named Marie Nightingale, an obvious alias. Marie claimed to have been kidnapped and held prisoner for years before her daring escape. Night after night, she captivated Ellie and her audience with her harrowing tales. Once a connection had been established based on their histories, Marie started showing up on campus, insinuating herself into Ellie's circle of friends in order to ferret out information about her personal life and Riley's disappearance.

Tom had eventually uncovered the woman's real identity and her true motivation. By then, however, she'd already published a sensational, mostly fictional book on the kidnapping, calling into question Ellie's innocence and tainting Tom's reputation in the process. Why had Ellie been the only one of the three friends to escape Preacher's clutches that night? And how convenient that her brother had been able to save her but not the other two girls.

Melanie Kent wasn't the only one who'd harbored those dark suspicions. When Tom had discovered that Ellie and her friends had snuck out of the house that night, he'd rushed out to the Ruins to find them, only to be ambushed and also left for dead on the banks of Echo Lake. Regaining consciousness, he'd had to make the tragic choice of searching for the missing girls or rushing his sister to the ER. His actions had likely saved Ellie's life, but there were still doubters in town that held to the notion both Tom and Ellie had abandoned Riley and Jenna in order to save themselves.

It had taken a lot of years and a very thick skin to live down the ugly innuendoes. Which was why Ellie had been reluctant to call Tom earlier, why she hated dragging him into a situation that might stir bad memories and bitter feelings. The Cavanaughs weren't the only family that had been put through the wringer by Riley's disappearance.

"I've made some inquiries," Tom said. "Melanie was recently fired from the publication she worked for in Tyler and before that she was let go from the *Dallas Herald*. I'm guessing that's why she's sniffing around Belle Pointe again."

"You think she's behind these calls?"

"I wouldn't put anything past her, especially if she's desperate. She was always a ruthless and ambitious reporter. It wouldn't be the first time she cooked up an outlandish scheme to get a story or a book deal."

"I wish you'd told me sooner," Ellie said again worriedly.

"Yeah, me, too. I should have told you the minute I heard she was back in town. That was my mistake."

"Don't keep something like that from me again."

"I won't." He paused, looking discomforted.

"What?" Ellie pressed. "What else aren't you telling me?"

"Nothing about Melanie, I swear. But if it's all the same to you, I'd rather Rae not know about the phone calls or the woman you saw by the lake. At least not yet."

"You think it's a good idea to keep secrets? She's bound to find out sooner or later," Ellie warned.

"I know, but after everything she and her family have been through, I want her to enjoy all the wedding preparations without having the specter of her sister's kidnapping hanging over her. I say we keep a close eye on things and see if we can put a stop to this nonsense quietly."

"Fine by me," Ellie said.

"Meanwhile, I'll keep digging and see if I can find out what Melanie Kent is really up to."

"You do that, Tom."

His gaze deepened. "I don't think there's anything to worry about, but promise me you'll take precautions. Lock the studio door when you're on the air. Secure the house when you get home. And call me night or day if you hear or see anything suspicious or troublesome."

"I will. Let's hope whoever is behind this has had their fun and nothing else will happen. But, Tom…" She closed her eyes on a breath. "What if it isn't someone playing a cruel joke or a sleazy reporter after a story? I'm not saying I think Riley is still alive or anything, but what if that caller really is in trouble?"

"Then why wouldn't she go to the police?"

"Maybe she can't for some reason. I don't know," Ellie said helplessly. "I just need to make sure for my own peace of mind that I've done all I can."

"I understand. We'll get it all sorted out, I promise."

Ellie nodded, but she couldn't shake a lingering

unease that something darker than a prank may have motivated those phone calls.

THEY SPENT AN hour examining footprints and tramping through the woods, searching for additional evidence left by the predawn visitor. Coming up empty-handed, Tom reluctantly headed back into town and Ellie set out for the Thayer place to feed the peacocks.

She told herself she wouldn't dwell on the motivation behind those phone calls or the reason some strange woman had been staring up at her bedroom window. Maybe she really had imagined the whole episode. She recalled vividly the disturbing phone conversation that had come after the sighting, but already the figure at the water's edge seemed hazy and surreal.

It wouldn't be the first time she'd seen or heard something that wasn't really there. She'd been plagued by nightmares and hypnagogic visions for years. In some ways a figment of her imagination might be the preferable explanation. A flesh-and-blood intruder was a whole different worry. The notion that she might be the target of a stalker or even a malicious prankster chilled her more deeply than she wanted to admit.

A strutting peacock greeted her with an eerie scream. The peahens were less noisy as they gobbled up the grain and seeds she tossed out to supplement their diet of insects and berries. As always, the male wanted her to know that she had intruded upon his domain. He fanned his magnificent tail feathers before picking his way to the edge of the embankment where he turned to watch her with avid curiosity.

She sat down on the porch steps and let her mind wander for a few minutes. She needed to get home and start her workday, yet she lingered, as if that swaggering peacock could somehow protect her from what was coming. A smaller male joined the peahens pecking in the dirt. He was only too happy to strut his stuff until the older and larger male made his way back into the circle. Then the younger one retreated to the perimeter to nibble on wild grapes.

Ellie didn't know how long she'd been sitting there, lost in thought, when a prickling at the back of her neck brought her head up to search her surroundings. She didn't see anything amiss, but the peafowl scattered. Someone was coming through the woods.

Her first thought was that Adam Thayer, the owner of the property, might have returned from Dallas. Or maybe his girlfriend, Nikki Dresden, had come over to check on the place in his absence. But Ellie hadn't heard a car. She kept her gaze fixed on the overgrown driveway, hoping to see a familiar figure appear through the lush vegetation.

All was still. Even the mild breeze had died away. Yet she knew with dreaded certainty that she was no longer alone.

She rose, clutching the banister as she scanned the woods and then glanced down toward the lake. A boat bobbed alongside the dock. Had the small vessel been there when she arrived? She would have heard an outboard motor, but she'd been so lost in thought, she might have missed someone paddling up. They could have tied off quietly and slipped through the woods to watch her.

As many times as Ellie told herself she had no reason to worry, the whispery warning came back to haunt her. The unknown caller had tapped into her greatest fear. Buried deep down in her subconscious was the gnawing terror that Preacher would someday return for her. Rationally, she knew her brother was right. That particular monster was long dead or imprisoned. Even if he still roamed free, he was an old man now. Why would he risk coming back here to torment her?

Because you're the one that got away.

But she hadn't gotten away. Not really. She and the other two girls had separated that night in the Ruins. Riley had been terrified from the start. She'd clutched Jenna's arm as the two stood at the bottom of the stairs and watched Ellie ascend to the second floor. Halfway up, she'd regretted her bravado, but she was too proud to turn back even when Riley had pleaded with her to come down.

If we're going to do this, we need to stick together, Elle.

Don't be such a worrywart, Riles. It's just an old building. Nothing to be afraid of. Why don't you come up here with me?

Not a chance.

Fraidy-cat.

Leave her alone, Ellie. We should never have brought her out here in the first place.

You wanted to come, didn't you, Riles?

I...guess so.

See there, Jen? Now you're *the worrywart.*

No, I'm just being a good friend. Unlike you, who never thinks about anyone but herself.

Stop it, both of you! Let's just get this over wi— What was that?

What was what, Riles?

I heard something.

Probably just a floorboard settling.

No, she's right, Ellie. Someone's here...

The memory floated away as Ellie came down the porch steps slowly. Sunlight shimmered on the surface of the lake, but the thick canopy of pine trees in the yard blocked all but a few anemic rays. A moment ago, the air had been still, but now a breeze riffled through the leaves, stirring the pungent scent of the evergreens and something that might have been cigarette smoke.

Ellie started to call out, but the paralyzing fear of her dreams held her back. For a moment, she stood rooted to the spot, unable to scream, unable to flee, unable to do anything but imagine the demonic face of her nemesis peering at her through the shadows.

Panic gripped her. She tried to focus on the sparkle of sunlight on the water. So pretty. Like diamonds. *Focus on the diamonds...*

She concentrated on taking slow deep breaths until the paralysis lifted and she could put one foot in front of the other. It seemed to take an eternity to cross the yard to the embankment, but then she descended too quickly, turning an ankle on the wooden steps and scraping her knees when she fell.

Scrambling to her feet, she hurried the rest of the

way down and paused at the edge of the dock to study the small fishing boat. She didn't see any oars, couldn't tell if the boat had been there all along or not. Adam Thayer owned one very much like it. She'd seen him tooling across the lake on several occasions. He'd probably removed the small outboard to store in a safe place while he was away.

See? A logical explanation. Nothing to be afraid of. You've come here dozens of times to feed the peacocks—

Her thoughts scattered on a gasp when she saw someone at the top of the embankment.

A man stood in shade so deep that Ellie had only an impression of a human form. She told herself it was nothing. Just a shadow. A tree or a bush. *No one is there.*

He moved up to the edge of the ridge. Slowly. Stepping into thinner shade but not venturing out into full sunlight. He was dressed in a black suit and he wore an old-fashioned parson's hat pulled low over his face. Someone had painted a mural of Preacher on the ceiling of the Ruins, distorting his features into a demonic grimace beneath the brim of a similar hat.

It was that evil face that had terrorized Ellie's sleep for years, whereas she could barely remember Silas Creed, a former mental patient who had once worked odd jobs in town. He'd disappeared on the night of the kidnapping. No one had seen or heard from him since. No one knew what had happened to him, though there'd been claims of sightings from time to time. Some swore he was still hiding out nearby, foraging and stealing to get by. Some insisted he'd died a long time ago and his ghost now haunted the Ruins. Ellie tried not to think about him at all, but there he stood…there *someone* stood…

He's not real. He's not real. He's not real.

Sunlight glimmered down through the pine bowers, bathing his dark-clad form in a soft glow that made her wonder for a moment if she really was seeing a ghost.

He didn't glance her way. Didn't once make eye contact. He merely stood there with his head bowed as if in deep prayer or contemplation.

Something splashed in the water and Ellie whirled toward the dock. The noise distracted her for only a split second, but when she turned back around, the figure had vanished.

The pungent smell of smoke grew stronger. Ellie scanned the embankment, worried that he might have somehow descended without her seeing him. Then she turned back to search along the tree line as she tried to calculate the fastest way home. The road would be quicker, but she'd have to go back up the steps, across the yard and down the tree-shrouded drive to the gravel lane. Maybe she should climb into the boat and push off so that she could drift out into the middle of the lake where she could see in every direction—

Just go!

Heart pounding, she rushed headlong down the trail toward home. A flock of snowy egrets took flight, startling her so badly she almost went down a second time. She righted her balance and kept moving. Rounding the final bend, she finally glanced over her shoulder to make sure the coast was clear.

That was a mistake. When she whirled back around, he stood on the path, blocking her escape.

Chapter Three

Ellie threw up her arms and braced herself, prepared to go down fighting if she had to. Her law enforcement dad had also taught her self-defense. However, no action was needed in this case. The man on the path stepped out of the way at once, but the adrenaline still pumped so furiously through Ellie's veins that she had the primal urge to lash out. He must have glimpsed something in her eyes that startled him because he took another step back. "Whoa, there. You okay?"

He wasn't the man she'd seen on the embankment. He wasn't dressed in black, didn't wear a hat and he was too young to be Preacher. Ellie tried to calm herself enough to reassess the situation as she glanced over her shoulder. The trail behind her was clear, thank goodness.

She took a moment to catch her breath as she turned back to the newcomer. He was tall, fit, late thirties maybe. Dark hair. Dark eyes. Charcoal trousers, white shirt open at the neck and rolled up at the sleeves.

"You shouldn't sneak up on someone like that," she admonished, as the adrenaline rush subsided.

"I generally don't make a habit of it." He sounded the tiniest bit defensive. "You came around that bend in such a hurry I didn't have time to get out of your way."

Ellie threaded her hair behind her ears as her heart rate gradually returned to normal. Had she really seen someone at the top of the embankment or had the black-clad figure been another figment of her imagination?

Now that she was out of danger, self-doubt crept in and she wasn't sure why. It was broad daylight and she was wide-awake. She hadn't dreamed up that shadowy form in the hat any more than she'd imagined the woman by the lake. Both were real, which meant someone was deliberately tormenting her. But why?

"Are you sure you're okay?" the stranger asked.

She snapped back to the present, lifting her gaze to meet his. His eyes were dark and piercing. Unnerving under the circumstances.

"I'll be a lot better when you tell me who you are and what you're doing out here." She took in his casual business attire once more. Not a sight she often saw on the banks of Echo Lake. Her gaze narrowed. "Wait a minute. I know you."

He held up a hand as if to reassure her of his benevolence, then slowly reached back with the other hand to retrieve his credentials from his pocket. "Agent Sam Reece."

The name hit Ellie like a sledgehammer blow. Another person from her past. Another face from her nightmares.

Oh, did she ever know Agent Samuel Reece. She remembered only too well his endless questions after

Riley had gone missing. The flashes of skepticism and impatience when Ellie hadn't been able to give him the answers he wanted. She'd thought him arrogant and aggressive back then. Ruthless in his quest to uncover the truth no matter who got in his way. Under most circumstances, his resolve would have been appreciated, but he'd made no bones about his concern that the county sheriff might be covering for his daughter.

"What do you want?" The question came out far terser than she'd intended, but instead of offering an apology, she lifted her chin in defiance.

"I'd like to ask you a few questions if that's okay." Those fathomless eyes observed her with open curiosity. He was an attractive man. She remembered that about him, too. The years had only enhanced his good looks with an air of quiet confidence that wore more easily than the previous sharp edges. Fifteen years was a long time. People did change, but it was too risky to give him the benefit of the doubt.

Ellie said coolly, "Do you think my answers will be any different than they were fifteen years ago?"

He shrugged. "Probably not. This isn't about fifteen years ago. I'm here about the call that came into your radio show last night."

She stared at him in astonishment. "How do you know about that?"

"I listen to your program from time to time."

She didn't know which revelation disturbed her the most—that he'd come about the call or that he listened to her show. The notion that he'd kept tabs on her all these years unsettled her.

"I find the subject matter fascinating," he added.

"Which subject matter in particular?" she shot back.

"I enjoy all the shows, but I'm partial to the ones on unsolved mysteries."

"Yes, I can see how that topic would interest you." Ellie brushed past him as she moved toward the steps. "Maybe you should come on the program sometime. I could interview you for a change."

"Name the night."

She turned. "You're serious?"

A smile flickered as he shrugged. "Why not? I should probably warn you, though, that I'm hardly a polished speaker."

"Somehow I doubt that," she muttered, scouring the shadowy trail once more. If anyone had followed her from the Thayer place, that person was either long gone or in hiding. Maybe she had Agent Reece to thank for that. She let her gaze roam along the tree line before she glanced back.

"Are you sure you're okay?" he pressed. "You seem nervous. Just now when you came along the bank, you looked frightened. Did something happen?"

Who better to confess her fears to than an FBI agent? But this particular agent had once accused her of hiding something. The last thing she wanted was to trigger a new round of suspicions, so she decided to say nothing until she learned the real reason for his unexpected visit.

"I'm fine," she said briskly. "If you're here to interrogate me, we may as well go up to the house where we can be comfortable. But I've work to do so I don't have a lot of time."

Something flashed in his eyes, an emotion she found hard to define. If she didn't know better, she might have thought it remorse.

"No interrogation, just a few simple questions," he said. "I'll try to be brief."

He followed her up the steps to the shady deck. Instead of inviting him into the house, she motioned to one of the chairs that faced the water. "Have a seat. I'll bring out some coffee. Or would you prefer iced tea?" The sun was already hot and she was still perspiring from her mad dash back home, but it was comfortable and breezy in the shade. She wished she had nothing more pressing than a leisurely morning on the deck, wished she had the nerve to send Agent Reece packing. But curiosity niggled. Why was he really here?

"Coffee is fine, thanks." Ignoring the chair, he went over to the edge of the deck and stared out across the water. His dark hair was cut short, though it seemed a little longer than she remembered. When he turned his head just right, she could see the barest glimmer of frost at his temples.

She tore her gaze away from his profile.

"This is nice," he said. "Peaceful. I'd forgotten how beautiful Echo Lake is."

"By day, yes. When the sun goes down, it gets really dark with all the trees. Some people find it spooky."

"Yet you live out here anyway."

"I'm used to the dark. And as you said, it's a beautiful place." If one didn't look too hard for the monsters.

He turned at that. "It's good to see you again, Ellie."

The familiar way he used her first name unnerved

her. She felt the flutter of something halfway between fear and attraction in the pit of her stomach.

His gaze swept her house and the wooded landscape. "It seems you've done well for yourself."

"I've done okay."

He seemed at a loss for a moment. "I know I came on strong back then. It was my first big case. I was inexperienced, obsessive and we were up against a ticking clock. Every second that went by counted. So I pushed you to remember details. Probably harder than I should have, considering what you'd been through. But it was never personal."

"It felt personal."

"Then I apologize. I've wanted to tell you that for a long time."

Ellie didn't know whether to believe him or not. She *wanted* to. He looked and sounded sincere, but she told herself not to let down her guard. Not yet. She'd been taken in one too many times by consummate actors. People looking for a story, looking for an angle, looking to trip her up. She liked to think she'd learned from her mistakes.

"All I ever wanted was for Riley to come home," she said.

"That's what we all wanted."

She started to say something else, then turned and went inside the house. Her view of the deck from the kitchen window allowed her to discreetly study Agent Reece as she prepared a fresh pot of coffee. Whenever she'd thought about him over the years, she'd always remembered his eyes. In her mind, they were cold, black and fathomless, but in reality they were a deep, intense blue, almost navy. Earlier, she'd noticed the addition of worry lines at the corners and something indefinable lurking beneath the surface that made her wonder about his past.

He must have seen some pretty terrible things in the fifteen years since they'd last met. He hunted missing children and the monsters that took them. A job like his could change a person in ways most people could barely comprehend, but that didn't mean he got a pass from her. That didn't mean she ever had to trust him again.

She ran a hand through her messy hair, wondering if she should take the time to brush out the tangles. Maybe even change from shorts into jeans so that she didn't feel quite so exposed. Then she shrugged and thought, *To hell with that*. She wasn't a frightened, traumatized kid anymore. She could handle a few questions without needing to don armor.

He heard her footsteps and strode over to open the door. Waving aside his offer of help, she handed him a steaming mug and once again motioned to the chairs.

Across the lake, a family of white-tailed deer drank at the water's edge, but the idyllic setting did little to calm Ellie's trepidation. Why was he here?

Reluctantly she returned her focus to the man beside her. "So you were listening to my program last night," she prompted.

"That surprises you?" He took a tentative sip.

"Astounds me, actually. How did you even know about my show? I occupy a very small niche on the airwaves."

"Not as small as you might think. You have a devout following. Word gets around."

"All the way to DC?"

"I'm not in DC anymore. I'm back in Dallas."

She tried not to show her alarm. He was that close? "Since when?"

"Recently."

Ellie set aside her cup and folded her arms protectively. "Let's quit beating around the bush. Why don't you just tell me why you're really here? Why now, after all this time? Surely there's more to your visit than a few prank phone calls. Has something new turned up? You haven't..." She trailed off.

"Haven't what?"

She could barely bring herself to say it. "Found remains."

"No, nothing like that." He set aside his cup, as well. "Before we go any further, I should make one thing clear. I didn't personally hear your show last night. Someone told me about the caller. And you're right. That's not the only reason I'm here."

"Who told you about the caller—" Ellie broke off as something occurred to her. She felt a surge of anger as she studied his features. "You've been in touch with Melanie Kent, haven't you? That's why you're here. Both of you coming back to Belle Pointe at the same time can't be a coincidence. What has she told you?"

He said in confusion, "I'm sorry. I don't know what you're talking about. I don't know anyone named Melanie Kent."

"Of course you do. She interviewed you for a book

she wrote about Riley's disappearance. *I always thought the Brannon girl was hiding something.* Your exact words, I believe. That quote was picked up by all the local news outlets. You have no idea how long it took me to live it down."

He had the grace to look discomfited. "She took that quote out of context."

"So you do remember her."

"Vaguely."

Ellie nodded. "Now it's all starting to make sense. Melanie Kent turns up back in town after all these years and I start getting strange phone calls. And here you are. If I didn't know better, I might think she'd orchestrated everything."

"I can assure you I haven't talked to Melanie Kent or any other reporter about the Cavanaugh case in years. If I recall correctly, what I really said was—"

"I don't care what you said," Ellie cut in. "I'm only interested in why you're here."

"I'm here because Jenna Malloy is convinced the person calling into your radio program is Riley."

Ellie stared at him in shock. "You've talked to Jen? When?"

"Last night after she heard your broadcast."

Ellie hardly knew what to make of this new information. Jenna had notified the FBI about the mysterious caller? And Agent Reece had taken her seriously enough to drive out to Echo Lake? "You can't possibly think Riley is still alive."

"The chances are slim," he admitted. "But it seems Jenna has also been getting phone calls. Last night, someone left a peacock feather on her front porch. She thinks Riley is trying to send her a message."

A *peacock* feather? "Why would she think that?"

"She said peacocks were their thing. Hers and Riley's."

"No, peacocks are my thing," Ellie said. "Riley was afraid of them. She didn't like the sound they made at night. She said the screams gave her nightmares. Why would Jenna tell you that peacocks were their thing?"

"She seems to think the feather has meaning only to her."

Ellie said carefully, "I've kept in touch with Jenna over the years. Not as often as I should, but I know she still has a lot of issues. Understandable after everything she went through."

He nodded, his gaze somber. "I'm aware of those issues. We've kept in touch over the years, as well."

They'd kept in touch. He and Jenna.

Ellie didn't know what to make of any of this. She suddenly felt disconnected, as if she'd awakened from a long, deep sleep only to find that a lot of troubling things had occurred while she slumbered.

That's what you get when you hide out for too long. You lose track of time and people.

She gave him a doubtful glance. "I find that strange since I've never heard her mention your name."

His gaze on her remained steady. "How often do the two of you talk?"

"Often enough to know this isn't the first time she's imagined Riley reaching out to her."

"Yes, but something seems different this time."

"Different how?"

He hesitated. "Nothing I can define at the moment. I haven't talked to her in person. Maybe once we meet, I'll have a better handle on the situation."

Ellie found herself gripping the arms of her chair. She flexed her fingers, forcing her muscles to relax. "I still don't understand why you've come to see me."

He got up and went back over to the edge of the deck, leaning against the railing as he faced her. He was even taller than she remembered. Still intimidating, though she didn't like to admit it. She took a few steadying breaths, careful not to inhale so deeply that he'd notice.

"I wanted to get your take on the phone conversation before I talked to Jenna," he said.

"It wasn't much of a conversation. The connection was poor and I kept getting a lot of interference in my ear."

"You didn't recognize the voice?"

Now Ellie was the one who hesitated. "It was a very brief staticky call."

"What did the caller say?"

"'He's coming.'"

"Nothing else?"

"Nothing that I could make out. I assume you explained to Jenna that if by some miracle Riley is still alive and has somehow managed to get away from her captor, she'd go to the police or her family instead of taking the time to call into a talk radio show."

"I did. And Jenna reminded me that after fifteen years in captivity, Riley might not be able to think rationally."

Ellie glanced away, shivering in the heat as dark images floated through her head. She closed her eyes, trying to block out the bits and pieces of horror. "You *can't* believe she's still alive."

"As I said, the chances are slim."

"Yet you came all this way because of a phone call."

"The case has never been closed. We continue to follow leads as they come in."

"How often is that?"

"Rarely these days." He planted his hands on the railing and leaned back. He appeared infuriatingly at ease as Ellie's heart continued to thud. She turned to scan the lake, keeping Agent Reece in her periphery. Fifteen years ago he'd been fresh out of Quantico, an ambitious young agent out to make a name for himself at her expense. And now? She couldn't get a good read on him. Did he really believe Riley could still be alive or was he here because he remained suspicious of Ellie?

She needed to keep him talking for a bit, find out what he was really after before she sent him away. But she had to tread carefully with Special Agent Reece. He was older, wiser and despite his calm demeanor, probably a lot more cynical.

"I suppose Jenna also told you about the other calls that came into my program on two previous nights. They came in at roughly the same time, but the reception was so poor I couldn't make out the caller's voice until last night."

"What do you think is going on with these calls?" he asked.

"The truth? I think they're part of an elaborate hoax. A sick prank. Ever since Sophie Cavanaugh's kidnapping several weeks ago, Riley's disappearance has been all over the news. The rehashing always provokes calls from people claiming to have seen her. Or claiming to be her."

"How often has that happened?"

"A few times over the years. The Cavanaughs are important people around here. Whenever one of them makes the news, the kidnapping is invariably brought up."

He nodded thoughtfully. "I assume you have a recording of last night's broadcast? I'd like to listen to the portion with the phone call, if you don't mind."

"I don't mind, but you won't learn much."

"I'd still like to hear it. I'd also like for you to walk me through the rest of your night."

She frowned. "Why?"

"I'm trying to fill in the blanks," he said. "I'd like to get a sense of your routine. You don't have to tell me anything you'd rather I not know."

What did he mean by *that*? Was he still implying she had something to hide?

"I signed off the air, locked up the studio and came home."

He nodded behind her to the long row of windows. "The studio isn't in your house?"

"It's just down that path." She pointed toward the bottom of the steps.

"Convenient to have it so close," he remarked.

"The beauty of modern technology."

His tone and expression remained impassive despite a dark glimmer in his eyes. He was still looking to her for answers, but nothing good came from pawing around in all those fractured memories. Silas Creed was long gone, long dead. Nothing else mattered.

She lifted her chin, giving him an answering scrutiny and took a measure of petty satisfaction when he looked away first.

He glanced down the deck steps toward the path. "So after the call came in, you locked up the studio and came home. What then?"

"I took a shower and got ready for bed."

He gave a vague nod as if his mind had gone elsewhere. Then he turned to face her. "I'm curious about something. Why would you label a few staticky phone calls an elaborate hoax? Elaborate implies multiple layers and accomplices."

She should have been more circumspect with her wording, Ellie realized. But did it really matter in the long run? She remembered only too well Agent Reece's perception and doggedness. If he sensed she was holding something back, he'd keep poking and prodding at her defenses until weariness finally let him in.

"After my shower, I went downstairs to watch TV," she said. "I fell asleep on the couch. The doorbell woke me sometime later, but no one was there. Then just before dawn, I got up again and saw a woman at the edge of the lake. She seemed to be staring up at my bedroom window. She disappeared into the woods and a few minutes later, I received another call on my cell from someone claiming that Preacher was coming back for me. Just now? Just before I ran into you on the path? I saw someone dressed in black wearing a parson's hat. You know what that is, right? It's the same style depicted in the ceiling mural at the Ruins. Is all that elaborate enough for you, Agent Reece? And that's not even taking into account everything going on with Jenna."

He straightened from the railing as he gazed down at her. "Is there a reason you didn't tell me any of this earlier?"

"You took me by surprise. I wasn't expecting to bump into you on the trail."

He looked as if he wanted to press her with more questions about the *hoax*, but then relented. "Fair enough. Do you think the calls are coming from the same person?"

"I assume so, but I can't be sure." She glanced down where her fingers were once again clutching the arms of her chair.

"Can you describe the woman you saw by the lake?"

"Light hair, slender, about my height or a little taller. I really didn't get a good look at her. She was too far away and the shadows were too deep along the bank."

"What about the man in the parson's hat?"

"I never saw his face."

"Is it possible they could be the same person?"

The notion took Ellie by surprise. "I suppose so. Come to think of it, the build was similar." She paused. "What are you getting at, Agent Reece?"

"Nothing specific. I'm still trying to figure some things out."

"That makes two of us," Ellie said. "The only thing I can tell you for certain is that neither of them was Riley Cavanaugh."

Chapter Four

Sam watched the flicker of emotions across Ellie's face as she queued the recording. He knew her voice so well from her radio show that he had to remind himself she was a virtual stranger. He hadn't seen her in years and she looked a lot different than he remembered. That was to be expected, of course. She was an accomplished woman now rather than a traumatized teenager. An attractive woman, if he were honest, but still defensive and evasive. Still holding onto her secrets.

She glanced up reluctantly. "Take as much time as you need. I've work to do back at the house. Just lock up when you're finished."

"Thanks."

She nodded and looked as if she wanted to say more, but instead turned and left the studio. He could see her through the large picture window that looked out on the wooded trail. He followed her progress along the path until she disappeared into the lush vegetation near her deck. Even then he stared after her for a moment longer before returning his attention to the task at hand. Slipping on the headphones, he pressed Start and adjusted the volume. Then he played the recording all the way through her sign-off and hit Repeat.

He'd heard Riley Cavanaugh's voice from videos supplied by her friends and family at the time of her disappearance. Could the caller really be her? Nearly impossible to fathom after all this time and yet Sam couldn't deny a vague familiarity that may or may not have been his imagination. Had he heard this voice before?

After a few more listens, he removed the headphones, turned off the equipment and exited the studio.

Shading his eyes, he gazed across the shimmering water. Spanish moss rippled in the mild breeze as yellow water lilies unfurled in the heat. It was a beautiful clear morning now that the mist had burned off. He took a moment to appreciate the primal beauty of the landscape before lifting his head to trace the old smokestack that rose up through the treetops.

He hadn't been to the Ruins in years, but during those first few weeks of the investigation, he'd spent a lot of time going from room to room, searching through the rubble, sometimes just standing quietly in the shadows as he tried to visualize what had happened. He thought about heading over there now, but he wasn't quite finished with Ellie Brannon.

She was seated at a table on the deck with her laptop. When she heard him on the steps, she closed the lid and glanced up expectantly. Her eyes were a beautiful light blue, almost crystalline even in the shade. She'd brushed her hair while he was gone, pulling the blond strands back into a smooth ponytail that glistened in the morning light. She wore a white T-shirt over jean shorts, and Sam's gaze dropped to her tanned legs for a split second before he caught himself. *Don't even think about it.*

Those shimmering eyes seemed to note his attention as she lifted her chin. "Well?"

He strode across the deck and took a seat across from her at the table. "I'd like to have the recording analyzed if you've no objection. If we can filter out enough of the noise, we may be able to pick up something in the background."

She pushed aside the laptop and folded her arms on the table. "You can do with it what you want, but why waste time and resources? Surely you've more pressing cases."

He said carefully, "I doubt Riley's family would consider it a waste of time and resources."

Her voice sharpened. "I hope you're not planning to talk to them about any of this. At least not yet. It seems unnecessarily cruel to get their hopes up."

"Don't you think they have a right to know?"

"Know what?" she demanded. "That some awful person has come out of the woodwork to torment Jenna and me?"

"The incidents you've both described take planning and coordination. I think we can safely say this has gone beyond the prank stage."

"Then what do you think is going on?" Fear shadowed her eyes as her fingers curled around the chair arms. She was a lot more anxious than she wanted to let on, Sam thought.

He tried to remain cool. The last thing he wanted

to do was worry her, but if his hunch was correct, she needed to be on guard. "Do you have any enemies or professional rivals? Someone who would want to damage your credibility? Drive you off the air, maybe?"

"Radio is as cutthroat as any other entertainment medium, but in the scheme of things, my show is small potatoes. I keep my head down and do my best not to offend any listeners or tick off the suits. I'm comfortable in my niche with no ambition to move out of it. Besides, if the phone calls and visits are professionally motivated, why go after Jenna? That's rhetorical, by the way, as I suspect you've already made the same deduction."

He watched her closely. "Yes, but sometimes it's helpful to talk through various scenarios. Process of elimination."

She didn't look convinced. He could hardly blame her. He'd given her no reason to trust him in the past. Finesse and tact had been late additions to his investigative arsenal.

"Tell me more about this Melanie Kent," he said.

"There isn't much I can tell you. My brother said she'd been let go from the publication she worked for in Tyler, and before that, the *Dallas Herald*. He said she'd applied for a job with the local paper, but they turned her down."

"Sounds like she may be getting a little desperate."

Those crystalline eyes had taken on a peculiar glitter at the mention of Melanie Kent. "As unscrupulous as that woman was on her way up the ladder? I hate to think what she'd be willing to do for a story on her way down. I haven't personally spoken with her, but I do find it curious that all these incidents coincide with her return to Belle Pointe. Maybe she's trying to convince both Jenna and me that Riley is still alive so that she can finally write her sequel."

"I'll see if I can find out what she's up to," Sam offered.

"No need. My brother will take care of it."

"I can tap into resources that are unavailable to a county sheriff."

Ellie looked both annoyed and skeptical. "Is that really the job of the FBI?"

"Melanie Kent's name has come up in the course of my investigation. That makes her fair game in my book."

"Investigation? So I'm to take this as an official visit?" She seemed unduly disturbed by the prospect. Sam couldn't help wondering why.

"As I said, the case has never been closed."

"And you follow every lead as they come in. I know. I heard you." She held his gaze for a moment before glancing away. "You should probably talk to my brother anyway if you're planning on being in town for a while. Things will go a lot smoother for you here in Nance County if you alert him of your intentions."

"I'll do that," Sam said with a nod. "I learned the hard way it's not a good idea to get crossways with the Nance County sheriff." He'd had his differences with the first Sheriff Brannon. He'd just as soon not get off on the wrong foot with the current one. "I was sorry to hear about your dad," he added.

Ellie's head came up. "How did you know about my dad?"

"We kept in touch."

Her eyes widened at the revelation. "Why?"

"Mostly to share information. We both made it a point to keep apprised of anyone connected to the Cavanaugh case. If anything relevant came to either of our attention, we passed it on."

She was silent for a moment. "Is that why you listen to my show? To keep apprised of my whereabouts and activities?"

"It may have started out that way. Now I tune in because I enjoy your program."

"Somehow I find that hard to believe."

"Okay. Maybe I am still trying to learn something from your broadcasts," he admitted. "I don't think you're hiding anything, but I do believe it's possible something may come back to you."

She frowned. "After all this time?"

He didn't answer right away, but instead examined a bank of white clouds hovering over the pine forest before bringing his gaze back to her. Her eyes seemed too knowing, as if she could peer into his soul. He found her intensity strangely enticing. "Right after it happened, you said you didn't notice anything out of the ordinary until you heard one of the girls scream. Then you were grabbed from behind. You never got a look at your assailant. Never heard him speak."

"That's right."

"I believe that's what you think, but dissociative amnesia can be a tricky thing. Traumatic memories can be buried so deep it's like the event never happened. Then years later something can trigger a flashback. A nightmare maybe or a photograph. Even the sound of a voice."

"Or maybe I really didn't see or hear anything out of the ordinary that night," she said. "A possibility you never wanted to accept."

He waited another beat. "Have you ever considered hypnosis?"

"I've done more than consider it. I tried it once."

"When was this?" he asked in surprise.

"In college. I couldn't be put under."

"Do you know why?"

She shrugged but it almost seemed more like a shudder to Sam. "A natural resistance to losing control, I suppose. The reason really doesn't matter because the experts will tell you that hypnotic regression is unreliable. The subject's perception of events may or may not be accurate. Which is why forensic hypnosis is still highly controversial."

"That's all true," he agreed. "But under the guidance of a trained therapist, regressive hypnosis can be helpful. I've seen it work."

She sat back in her chair, physically withdrawing from the conversation. "That's great, but as I said, it didn't work for me. What would be the point now, anyway? Nothing will ever bring Riley back. Nothing will ever make Jenna whole again. It might only make things worse for her. And as for their captor..." She closed her eyes briefly. "I have to believe Silas Creed is dead.

He's not coming back and I doubt his remains will ever be found."

"You're that certain Creed took Riley? Even though you never got a look at your assailant?"

"Yes. I'm that certain."

Sam sat back, too, contemplating her expression as he tried to tread softly. "There was very little physical evidence tying him to the kidnappings other than a few fingerprints and fibers that could have been left in the Ruins at any time prior to the night in question. No DNA. No eye witness accounts placing him at the scene."

She tried to hide her reaction, but he saw her breath quicken. "So? That doesn't prove anything. Fifteen years ago, the CSI shows on television had already educated the public about DNA and trace evidence. He knew to be careful."

"Do you really think Silas Creed was that sophisticated?"

"He was educated. People seem to forget that about him because of the way he lived after he left the psychiatric facility."

"All right. But do you think he was *physically* capable of following you and your friends to the Ruins and rendering you unconscious with chloroform, which, incidentally, takes a lot longer than movies make it seem. You would have struggled with him. Then when your brother comes looking for you, Creed knocks him on the head, rolls both your bodies down the embankment and flees with presumably an unconscious Jenna and Riley, all without leaving much of a trail."

Fear and dismay glimmered in her eyes, but not surprise. The thought had crossed her mind, too, at some point but she still didn't want to believe it. She dug down deep. "If he wasn't guilty, why did he run? He disappeared without a trace after that night. No one ever saw or heard from him again."

"Maybe he knew that given his mental health history and proclivity for hanging out at the Ruins, he'd be a likely suspect. Every law enforcement officer in the state would be looking for him. Creed had family in the area. Your dad once told me that he'd always wondered if a friend or relative had helped Creed leave town because they were afraid he'd be blamed for something he hadn't done. After all, he would have been an easy patsy. A loner and former psychiatric patient who delivered fire and brimstone sermons to an invisible congregation at the Ruins. He was familiar with the property. Knew every way in and every way out. Think about it. Even the nickname Preacher helped demonize him."

"You sound as if you want him to be innocent." There was an edge of accusation in her tone.

"I only want the truth."

"Still, it would be a fairly substantial boost to your career if you were to solve the case after all this time. Not to mention all the accompanying publicity. You might even score a book deal yourself."

He tried not to take the insinuation personally. "Don't you want the case solved?"

"In my mind, it is solved."

"I get it," Sam said. "It's a scary proposition to think that the real kidnapper could still be out there somewhere. Even if he were still alive, Silas Creed would be getting on in years. A non-threat. But I'm not convinced he was capable of pulling off those kidnappings alone and neither was Sheriff Brannon. We both had to live with the very real possibility that he had an accomplice. Or that a lone unsub may have been right under our noses, someone also familiar with the Ruins and the ritualized practice of local teens daring each other to spend time out there. Someone a lot more devious and clever than Silas Creed." He paused. "Someone who may still reside in this area."

Her face went ashen despite her tan. He heard a tremor in her voice when she spoke. "And you think this person has suddenly decided to come after Jenna and me? *Why?* It's been fifteen years. Why torment us now?"

"You said yourself Riley's disappearance has been all over the local news this summer. Maybe it's awakened something inside him, a need that he's managed to subdue all these years. Or maybe he wants you off balance, wants you to appear unstable and your memory unreliable in case something does come back to you. I don't have the answers right now. That's why I'm here. That's why I needed to come back after all these years."

"No matter how many painful memories you have to dredge up? No matter who gets hurt in the process?"

He hardened his resolve at the raw emotion she tried to blink away. "If that's what it takes to get justice for Riley and closure for her family, yes. Don't you want that, too?"

"Of course I do!"

"Then work with me. Help me find the truth."

"How?"

"If hypnosis is out, we can try returning to the scene. Maybe something will come back to you if we retrace your steps."

The suggestion seemed to render her speechless.

"It'll be okay," he offered lamely.

She shot him a dark look. "That's exactly what I told Riley before we entered the Ruins that night."

Chapter Five

The rest of the day passed quietly for Ellie. No anonymous phone calls, no strange sightings, no visits from the FBI. She tried not to obsess on any of those things, especially her conversation with Sam Reece, as she prepared for the evening's broadcast.

Normally, she was good at compartmentalization, but Agent Reece's visit had opened a door, allowing old fears to creep back in. What if the perpetrator really was someone she knew, perhaps even someone she spoke to on a regular basis? What if he'd watched her from afar for fifteen years, hiding behind a familiar face until those dark urges had lured the monster inside him back into her orbit?

She tried to push the disturbing images back into their cages as she settled down in her office to work. Turning her chair so that she couldn't stare out the window, she opened her laptop and went over her notes. She had an interesting guest lined up for the evening's broadcast. They would be speaking remotely about his latest book on collective consciousness. Ellie knew the author's work so well that it was easy to jot down several bullet points to keep the conversation flowing.

If she wasn't on her game or the interview didn't go as expected, she could opt for opening the phone lines. Her listeners relished the interaction portion of the show. Ellie had always enjoyed their questions and contributions until she started hearing from the unknown caller. Now dread niggled as she left the house late that afternoon to walk the short distance to her studio.

The sun was just sinking beneath the pine trees, casting long shadows across the water. The woods seemed to close in on her. She peered anxiously through the trees before turning to scan the opposite bank.

The August air was hot and steamy, but Ellie shivered as she contemplated her isolated surroundings. The monster from her past was dead and gone, and the shadowy creatures from her nightmares couldn't hurt her. She could stand on the bank of Echo Lake, lift her gaze to the old smokestack that loomed up through the pine trees and not cower in dread. It was just an old artifact. Just an abandoned structure.

Then why haven't you gone back there?

She had, once or twice. In broad daylight. She'd stood in the arched entrance, visualizing the mural on the ceiling from photographs that had run in the local newspaper. The painting had been done sometime after Riley's disappearance, but the demonized depiction with a wide-brimmed hat pulled low over the red eyes was the way Ellie now pictured Silas Creed. It was the way most people in Belle Pointe thought of him, too.

Yet in reality, he'd been a slight, nondescript man,

ordinary in appearance except for the hard glitter of madness in his eyes. The fiery orations he delivered from the tumbledown psychiatric hospital had become legendary, but Ellie had never known anyone who had actually seen him at the Ruins, let alone heard any of his apocalyptic preaching.

Had he been falsely accused? Was Silas Creed a tragic and disturbed individual who had become an easy target for the town's rage? A convenient face for Ellie's fear?

She closed her eyes for a moment, searching her memories and sifting through remnants of her nightmares. She must have seen something that night, heard a sound other than the pounding of her own heartbeat. Had there been footfalls on the stairway? Creaking floorboards? A face peering down at her a split second before everything went black?

Someone had screamed, but she'd never known if it was Jenna or Riley. Ellie had raced back along the second-story corridor to peer over the banister, down into all those shadows.

Riles? Jen? Is everything okay?

When no one answered, she'd started down the stairs, quickly at first and then more slowly as fear dragged at her feet like quicksand.

Something was wrong. Something terrible. It was all Ellie could do not to run away, but she had to find her friends and make sure they were okay. She couldn't leave them here.

A scent came to her as she reached the bottom of the steps. Acrid and smoky, like a smoldering cigarette.

She couldn't tell where the scent came from, only that it burned her eyes and made her cough.

Lifting a hand to her throat, she forced herself to move forward, one step at a time...

Jenna? Riley? Where are you? Please answer me. If this is a joke...

Where were they? Where were *they? If something had happened to them, she would never forgive herself. This was all her fault...her idea to come out here. Riley hadn't wanted to come...she'd been so scared. Don't be a baby, Ellie had taunted. Of course, we're going. We've been dared. We have to go...*

Riles? You okay? Jenna?

Something lay crumpled on the floor in front of her. She thought at first it was a pile of old rags. But the rags moved...

Footsteps sounded behind her as the smell of smoke grew stronger...an arm came around her waist...something was pressed against her mouth and nose...she couldn't breathe...couldn't breathe...the room spun, her knees buckled...it happened so fast...

And then darkness...nothing but darkness...

Ellie let go of the memory with a gasp and the blackness gave way to the gilded colors of an East Texas sunset. She hadn't realized that she'd been standing with her eyes squeezed shut. Now she drank in the sights and scents of the piney forest, allowing her surroundings to ground her in the present. That terrible night at the Ruins was fifteen years behind her, yet her heart continued to pound as a dark cloud of panic loomed. *Breathe. Slowly in, slowly out. Now focus.*

She picked a spot on the opposite bank where sunlight glimmered down through the pine trees.

In... Out...

Already the water lilies were closing for the day. The cicadas came out, along with swarms of mosquitoes. The pink horizon deepened to scarlet and then softened to lavender as the sun dropped beneath the horizon.

In... Out...

Ellie's gaze was still focused like a laser on the opposite bank. She could have sworn she saw a boat tucked up behind the heavy curtains of Spanish moss that skimmed the surface of the lake. She put up a hand to shade her eyes as she peered across the water. A human shape took form through the silvery strands. A man was seated in a boat, head bowed, facial features obscured by the wide brim of his hat.

Her chest tightened. She felt lightheaded with fear. *Breathe!*

A mirage. That's all it was. A figment of her imagination summoned by the deepening shadows. Preacher had been so much on her mind that she'd conjured his ghost. He wasn't real. No one was there.

In. Out.

If one stared at the same place for too long, the light played tricks. Like the explosion of color behind the lids before one drifted off to sleep. Not real.

She said the affirmation aloud. "Not real." Again. "Not real!"

The sound of her voice bolstered her courage. "Hey! What are you doing over there?" The question echoed back to her across the water. She laughed shakily and kept right on talking to the shadows. “Yeah, you!”

No answer. No movement. Nothing but an illusion.

She held her position, even though she had the strongest urge to turn and dash back to the house, lock herself inside and call her brother. Or she might even call Agent Reece. Desperate times called for desperate measures.

Drawing another breath, she walked all the way down to the water’s edge, daring the mirage to paddle out into the fading light.

“Who are you?” she shouted across the lake. “What do you want?” Emboldened by the silence, she waved her arms. “Hey, you!”

You’re losing it, Elle. Yelling at shadows. Seeing things that aren’t there.

The countryside had gone silent at the sound of her voice. She heard nothing now but the lap of water against the bank. The light faded and the sky deepened as she stood there. The lake took on a mysterious shimmer.

“I’m not afraid of you!” she called out. “Know why? Because you’re not real!”

Something plopped in the water just beyond the mossy curtain. Ellie told herself it was just a frog or a fish or a turtle. Nothing human. Nothing monstrous.

Another tiny splash, followed by another and another as if someone beyond her view had skimmed a stone across the surface of the lake.

A memory nudged its way out of the fringes.

Not like that, Riles. Skim. Don't throw. It's all in the wrist. Here. Let me show you.

Plop, plop, plop.

Not a frog, not a fish, not a turtle. Someone was over there.

Ellie didn't call out now, but instead stood frozen in silence. Fear lifted the hair at her nape, and she wanted nothing so much as to glance over her shoulder, make sure nothing or no one had come up behind her on the trail. But she was afraid to take her gaze off that silvery curtain in case Preacher could somehow materialize at the water's edge and come for her.

She stared at the spot for another few minutes before bracing her shoulders and deliberately turning her back to the water. What had she hoped to accomplish by yelling across the lake like that? Did she really think Preacher—or Agent Reece's unsub—was sitting in a boat, watching her?

Ignoring the icy prickles up and down her spine, she forced herself to walk unhurried to her studio. Once inside, she calmly locked the door and moved around her console to the picture window that looked out on the lake.

Still nothing moved. *Because no one is there.*

The clattering of her ringtone shattered the hush of her soundproof studio. She glanced down in dread, expecting to see *Unknown Caller* on the screen, but instead her brother's name appeared. She answered at once.

"That was fast," Tom said. "Everything okay?"

"Yes, I'm in the studio getting ready for the show."

"This early? It's barely even sundown."

"Which goes to show how little you understand about what I do. I don't just show up at airtime and start talking, you know." How perfectly normal she sounded. She was glad Tom couldn't see her at that moment. She must still look a bit wild-eyed. Holding her hand out in front of her, she confirmed a slight tremor.

"I won't keep you," Tom said. "I'm just calling to check in."

"Thanks." She gripped the phone as she peered out the window. She could still see all the way across the lake even as twilight eased in from the woods, blending with the shadows to hide the predators. A mild breeze parted the Spanish moss, but she couldn't see anything or anyone inside the cocoon.

"I need to tell you something before I go," Tom said hesitantly.

His tone jerked her back from the water. "What?"

"It's not a big deal," he rushed to assure her. "But I promised not to keep anything from you. I had a visitor this afternoon. I understand he came to see you, too."

She let out a breath. "You mean Agent Reece. Yes, I saw him this morning. What did he have to say to you?"

"It was mostly a courtesy call, but he did ask if he could take a look at the Cavanaugh case files. He seemed particularly interested in Dad's notes. Apparently, he's decided to look into Riley's kidnapping again."

Ellie shivered. "I know."

"He told me about Jenna. He said she's been getting anonymous calls, too. And someone left a peacock feather on her front porch." Tom paused. "He also told me about the man in the hat you saw earlier at the Thayer place. Why didn't you call me?"

She tried to keep her tone relaxed. "Because I didn't want you rushing back out to the lake when you've more pressing duties to attend to. Nothing happened. It was just more of the same. Someone playing a prank. Or maybe I imagined the whole thing."

"You didn't imagine anything and you should have called me."

Her brother had a tendency to be overprotective and Ellie usually pushed back, but not today. "You're right. I'm sorry. I didn't think it necessary because I wasn't alone. I ran into Agent Reece on the way home. That's when he told me about Jenna. It seems she's convinced Riley is trying to reach out to us."

"We both know that's not possible," Tom said.

"Yet here Agent Reece is back in Belle Pointe." It was all she could do to suppress another shiver. "I'd like to say that I admire his dedication, but his presence is going to dredge up a lot of bad memories. A lot of bad feelings, too. He wasn't the most tactful interrogator."

"If he crosses a line, you let me know," Tom said.

"I can handle his questions. I just hate that Rae is going to be put through this again." Ellie moved away from the window and took a seat behind her console. "Tom, Agent Reece said something I can't get out of my head. He told me Dad had never been convinced that Silas Creed acted alone. Or that he was even guilty. Did you know they'd stayed in touch? He said they'd both kept apprised of everyone connected to the case and had shared information over the years. I had no idea. Dad never said a word."

"He didn't like bringing that stuff home," Tom said with a note of caution. "Especially anything pertaining to the Cavanaugh case. He didn't want to upset you."

Ellie tucked a loose strand of hair behind her ear. "I know. He wanted to protect me just like you do, but I hate being kept in the dark. I'm not as fragile as you seem to think."

"I don't think you're at all fragile," Tom protested. "I do think you're too damn hardheaded for your own good at times. But you're right about keeping things from you. That's why I called you as soon as Reece left my office."

"Thanks." Ellie got up and paced restlessly, avoiding the window that looked out on the woods and lake. The deepening shadows unnerved her. "He said Dad had considered the possibility that a friend or relative may have helped Silas Creed disappear because they were afraid he'd be blamed for the kidnapping. He was worried the real kidnapper might be someone local and that the person may even still live in the area. Tom..." She couldn't help glancing out the window. "Did you know about any of this?"

"I knew a lot of people were questioned back then and various theories were considered. That's standard procedure. Or should be. A good investigator does his best to avoid focusing in too early on any one suspect, especially when the evidence is circumstantial. It's too easy to get tunnel vision."

Ellie gripped the phone. "And yet neither of you

thought I needed to know about these other possibilities?"

"We didn't want to scare you. You were in a bad way after it happened. You almost died and your best friends were missing. We did what we could to protect you, and as time went on, we made sure you knew how to protect yourself. The last thing Dad wanted was for you to spend the rest of your life hiding behind locked doors or always looking over your shoulder. He wanted you to have a normal life."

"But what about you, Tom?"

"What about me?"

"Is that why you've always hovered?" Ellie asked. "Because you're afraid the kidnapper is still nearby?"

"I don't consider it hovering. I've looked out for you because I'm your brother."

"You didn't answer my question. Tell me the truth. Do you think Silas Creed was innocent?"

"I don't know, Ellie. That's the God's honest truth." She could picture him running his fingers through his hair as the crinkles around his eyes deepened. "I've been over that night in my head a million times and as much as I want to believe he's guilty and that he acted alone…who can say for certain? He did have relatives in the area. It's possible one or more of them helped him get out of town quietly."

"Do they still live around here?"

"His half sister died a few years back. Her son came back home and took over the family farm. I haven't seen or talked to him in years, though I understand he's added greenhouses and a nursery to the vegetable gardens. His property is located about ten miles south of here on Route 27, near Carlisle. His mother always avoided Belle Pointe after what happened. I guess Cory does, too."

"What's his last name?"

"Small."

Cory Small. The name rang a faint bell. "Does Agent Reece know about these relatives?"

"I'm sure he does. The half sister was questioned any number of times after Creed disappeared. Dad always felt sorry for her. She was a widow, trying to make a living in a physically demanding business. She had her hands full. As I understand it, Creed was in his twenties when the family had him committed. They couldn't handle him anymore. He remained in the hospital until the facility closed down in the eighties. By that time, his parents had died. His sister was his closest living relative. She helped him find jobs and a place to live, but she had Cory to look out for. She cooperated with the authorities to a certain extent, but family is family."

"Do you think she helped her brother leave town?"

"It's possible, although her resources were limited. It takes a lot of money and connections to make someone disappear without a trace. The truth is we may never know what happened to Silas Creed. Sometimes I think that might be for the best."

SAM LET HIMSELF into his darkened townhome and flipped on the light as he tossed his keys on the console table in the foyer. He was bone-deep tired and he wasn't sure why. Maybe revisiting the Cavanaugh case wore more heavily on him than he'd anticipated.

Every missing child case haunted him, especially the ones that went unsolved. He'd long ago had to face the grim reality that some families would never find closure, much less peace. The Riley Cavanaugh case was different, not because it had been his first, but because of the nagging fear that he'd missed something. That his arrogance and inexperience had allowed a psychopath to go free all these years, one that may have kidnapped and murdered again.

He tried to shake off a creeping gloom. His office was on the ground floor and he thought about putting in a little extra time at his desk before calling it a night. There was always a case that needed more attention. Never enough manpower or hours in the day to get everything done.

Instead, he went straight upstairs to the kitchen and poured himself a drink. Then loosening his tie and shedding his jacket, he carried the whiskey out to the balcony and leaned a hip against the railing as he gazed off into the night.

His trip to Belle Pointe had stirred a lot of memories. He hadn't been back since he was pulled off the case three months into the investigation. On the surface, the place hadn't changed much, but the rose gardens and picturesque town square hid a lingering darkness. Sam had felt a strange oppression the moment he'd crossed the city limits. Fifteen years after her disappearance, the ghost of Riley Cavanaugh still haunted the shady streets.

He let his mind wander back to his conversation with Ellie Brannon. He couldn't seem to get her out of his head. He'd thought about her on the long drive back to Dallas and for the rest of the afternoon as he'd worked his way through a mountain of paperwork. Even now, hours later, the combination of exhaustion and good whiskey did little to dull his preoccupation.

He believed as he always had that Ellie held the key to solving the Cavanaugh case. Jenna Malloy's memories of her abduction and captivity were locked away forever. Her very survival depended on burying those memories deep. Ellie's experience was different. She hadn't been taken with the other two girls and that, too, remained a mystery. Sam didn't think she was deliberately holding anything back, but there was a chance she'd seen or heard something before she lost consciousness. Something long forgotten. Under the right circumstances, even seemingly innocuous details could still come back. The situation would have to be handled carefully, of course. He would need to slowly gain her trust.

He'd taken the first step today. Planted a seed. Under normal circumstances, she wouldn't be inclined to cooperate, but the sightings had her rattled. No matter how hard she tried to downplay everything that had happened she'd been terrified when he saw her on the trail that morning. Her fear would eventually demand answers, and Sam had long since learned the virtue of patience.

Meanwhile, he would clear his desk and head back to Belle Pointe as soon as his schedule allowed. Something was definitely going on down there. Something more than a prank or a vicious practical joke. Ellie Brannon was being targeted, and even though she had her brother to look out for her, Sam was surprised at how anxious he was to see her again.

Something stirred in the pit of his stomach and he took another sip, using the fire of the whiskey to avoid the inevitable. But the truth was right there, poking and prodding his resolve, demanding his acknowledgment.

The attraction had caught him by surprise. Who would have ever thought? Ellie had been a frightened kid when he'd last seen her. Wounded and lost and yet still defensive when he'd pushed her hard to remember. Now she was a grown woman. Tall, slim, blond with the clearest blue eyes he'd ever looked into. Deceptively clear, because like the town of Belle Pointe, the shadows of her past still lurked beneath the surface.

He couldn't help wondering what her life had been like for the past fifteen years. He knew the basics. An RTF major at the University of North Texas. A talk radio host in a niche market. Single. Never married. Lived alone on the lake.

His life hadn't turned out so different. He lived alone, lived for work. When he moved from DC to Dallas, he'd left behind a string of failed relationships with strong, attractive, successful women. Patient women who'd soon tired of his travel and long hours. Good women who'd eventually been repelled by the darkness that clung like a bad odor after every missing child case.

Ellie Brannon knew all about that darkness. She'd lived it.

That stirring again. A longing that made Sam shift uncomfortably at the railing. That made him peer harder than usual into the night, searching for monsters to quell his human needs.

Ellie was off-limits. Had to be off-limits. Even if she offered encouragement—which she wouldn't—he'd never make that move. After everything she'd been through, she deserved better. Not that he was a bad man. He wasn't. But he lived in the world of her nightmares. He was a good enough man to know that he was a bad match for someone like her.

Why was he even thinking about this?

Maybe he needed to get out of the house. Go out to a bar. Have a few drinks. Make a connection. Forget about the monsters and all those missing kids who paraded through his sleep at night, some he'd found and some he hadn't. Forget about Belle Pointe, Texas, and a missing girl named Riley Cavanaugh and her best friends, Jenna Malloy and Ellie Brannon.

He definitely needed a distraction. It was still early even for a weeknight and Dallas was a vibrant city. *Go have a drink and talk to some people. Remember what it's like out there in the real world.*

He went inside and put his glass on the counter before going back downstairs to grab his jacket. Driving alone at night, he kept his eyes peeled. The predators he hunted were out there even now, lurking around malls and movie theaters, watching from the shadows, watching through windows. Scoping out the easy victims.

Sam had learned to live with the bleak realities of his job, but even wide-awake, he'd never found a way to keep the nightmares at bay.

A few minutes later, he found a parking place and walked down the street to one of the few bars he'd visited since his return to Dallas. A lot had changed in fifteen years. The city sprawled in every direction and the traffic seemed endless. He glanced at faces on the street as he walked along, made eye contact now and then, murmured a greeting once or twice. It was good to be out and about. Or so he told himself.

The place was crowded and noisy. The beat of the music vibrated across his nerve endings as he took a seat at the bar and ordered another whiskey, sipping slowly as he observed the crowd in the mirror. He wasn't looking to hook up. Just needed to escape the darkness for a while. Needed to feel normal.

The crowd cleared after a while and a blonde seated alone at a table caught his eye. Slim, attractive. She reminded him of Ellie. He glanced away quickly before she got the wrong impression. Not tonight.

He sipped his drink and wondered if he should order another. He could always take a cab home and pick up his car in the morning. Or he could stop now and go get something to eat. He motioned to the bartender.

His phone rang and Jenna Malloy's name appeared on the screen. As always, he thought about letting the call go to voice mail, but he wouldn't. He never did. He took another sip of his drink, then pressed the phone to his ear in order to hear over the music.

"Hello?"

No answer.

"Jenna? Are you there?"

Someone was there. He could hear music and voices in the background. Then the call abruptly dropped.

He got up and walked outside, leaving his fresh drink on the bar. The evening was warm and clear. He leaned a shoulder against the building as he turned his face to the breeze, still fighting that odd restiveness.

His ringtone pealed again and he answered immediately.

"Jenna?"

"Hello, Agent Reece."

Apprehension prickled across his scalp. He didn't recognize the voice, yet it seemed uncannily familiar. "Who is this?"

A soft laugh.

He could still hear the pounding bass of the music but the sound was muted now. A horn blared on the street and in his ear. Sam's head came up as he glanced around, his senses heightened. He peered at passersby, looking for anyone on a cell phone, which seemed to be almost everyone.

"Who is this?" he repeated. "Why do you have Jenna's phone?"

"I wasn't sure you'd answer if I used mine."

He took a stab in the dark. "Hazel?"

"Very good, Agent Reece."

Jenna's new roommate. The prickling intensified. "Where's Jenna?"

"Oh…she's around."

"Put her on the phone. I'd like to talk to her."

"That's probably not a good idea right now."

"Why not?"

A pause. "She's not herself tonight."

Sam started walking, forcing a slow, easy gait as he searched for the caller. "What's that supposed to mean? Is she okay?"

"Don't worry about Jenny. She'll be back to her old self in no time. Our girl is nothing if not resilient, but I don't have to tell you that. You know exactly what she's been through, don't you, Agent Reece?"

"Why are you calling, Hazel?"

"I thought it a good opportunity for the two of us to talk."

"What do you and I have to talk about?"

"Aren't you curious about who Jenna is living with now? I'm certainly curious about you. She talks about you all the time. She's got quite a thing for you. I'm beginning to see why."

"Where are you, Hazel?"

Another soft laugh.

"Please have Jenna call me. I need to know she's okay."

"I told you, Jenna's fine. I'm more worried about you at the moment."

He paused and glanced around. "Why are you worried about me?"

"You look so lonely tonight."

Reflected headlights in a store window caught Sam in the face. After the vehicle passed by, he glimpsed someone standing on the curb across the street. A blonde with a phone to her ear.

He could have sworn the woman was Jenna Malloy, but when he turned, no one was there.

Chapter Six

Ellie didn't hear from the unknown caller on her show that night. The broadcast ended without a hitch and after she signed off the air, she removed her headphones and let out a breath of relief. Maybe whoever had been responsible for the calls had gotten bored with the prank and moved on.

But the anonymous calls were the least of her worries now. As much as she hated to admit it, Agent Reece was right. Everything that had happened took planning and coordination. Someone had gone to the trouble of finding out where she lived and memorized her daily routine. One hundred and sixty miles away, a peacock feather had been left on Jenna's front porch.

Was it possible the message behind the feather had been meant for Ellie? She was the one who had always loved peacocks. Not Jenna. Not Riley. The feather was symbolic, but of what?

The questions churned endlessly as she finished her nightly tasks. Pausing at the window, she peered out across the water, searching for a hidden boat, searching for shadows and monsters. No one was there. No one that she could see. Still, the notion of leaving the safe haven of her studio to walk the short distance to her deck filled her with dread.

Don't be ridiculous. If Tom thought you were in the slightest bit of danger, he would never have left you alone. You're fine. Go home, grab a shower and get some rest.

Maybe she'd make a cup of tea, something soothing and aromatic. A few days ago, she would have carried her drink out to the deck so that she could enjoy the night air, but now she anticipated sipping from the comfort of her bedroom with the downstairs doors locked tight and her weapon within easy reach.

She turned off all the lights and stood in darkness for a moment. Then hardening her resolve, she left the studio, locked the door and headed for home. An owl hooted from one of the pine trees as she hurried along the trail. The moon was up, casting a silver radiance over the path and wooded landscape, but the lake looked dark and forbidding.

Glancing over her shoulder, Ellie scanned the trees behind her. A breeze whispered through the leaves and feathered along her bare arms, raising goose bumps. She could smell something pungent on the wind, like the smoke from a distant campfire. Or a smoldering cigarette.

A thrill of fear shot through her. Someone was in the woods. She didn't see anything, didn't hear anything and yet she could feel someone watching her.

He's coming...

The warning echoed in her ears. She almost expected

to hear the peal of her ringtone at any moment from the same anonymous caller, but all was silent except for the excited thud of her heartbeat and the drone of a mosquito in her ear. She whirled and darted up the path, tripping in her haste to get home and scolding herself for her carelessness.

As she rounded the bend in the trail, she halted abruptly. What if instead of fleeing from someone behind her, she was running headlong into danger?

She turned her ear to the woods and then to the lake. Was that the hum of a distant outboard? The lap of water against a fiberglass hull? She swept the water. Why hadn't she brought one of the pistols with her when she left the house earlier? Why hadn't she stayed locked inside the studio until morning?

The darkness closed in on her from every direction as panic hovered.

She took a deep, calming breath and started forward. Her house was just footsteps away. She lifted her gaze to the bedroom window. She could have sworn someone stared down at her, but in the next instant, she realized the movement was just moonlight glinting off glass.

Fishing the key from her pocket, she hurried up the steps. The security lights illuminated the deck and grounds, but still the shadows encroached. She moved to the door, inserted the key and then froze yet again.

Someone had been on the deck while she was sequestered in the studio. The intruder had left a gift, something from Ellie's past that would only have significance to her and to Jenna… And to Riley.

Draped over the doorknob was a length of braided

red yarn similar to the friendship bracelets that had been popular for a brief time when Ellie, Jenna and Riley were in middle school. They'd made their bracelets together, weaving strands of each of their favorite colors into the plaits. Ellie's had been blue with intertwining single threads of yellow and red, Jenna's yellow with blue and red threads, and Riley's red with blue and yellow strands.

Ellie touched the faded yarn and an icy tingle shot up her arm. She snatched her hand away as another memory prodded. She tried to push the image away as she glanced frantically over her shoulder.

She wanted to leave the bracelet on the doorknob and pretend she'd never seen it, but when had burying her head in the sand ever been helpful? If someone was coming for her, she needed to be prepared.

Grabbing the braid, she hurried inside and locked the deadbolt behind her. She turned on the kitchen light and scurried down the hallway to check the front door. Satisfied the house was still secure, she went back into the kitchen, put the kettle on and only then did she uncurl her fingers to examine the bracelet under the light.

She told herself it was just a bit of faded yarn. It could have come from anywhere. But that wasn't really true. Even though the bracelet was worn and badly stained, she could still make out the single yellow and blue strands that had been woven into the red braid.

Gently, she placed the bracelet on the counter as memories swamped her.

Riley had worn her bracelet on the night they'd gone out to the Ruins. Ellie and Jenna had teased her about it, but she hadn't cared. She swore the braided band would protect her. The girls had agreed to stop wearing the bracelets when they left middle school. The crude jewelry had seemed too childish for high school. Ellie had tossed hers in the trash one night and then fished it back out the next morning. She couldn't bear to part with it. The interwoven threads signified the bond the girls had shared since kindergarten.

She'd kept that bracelet all these years in a secret compartment of her jewelry box, but she never looked at it anymore. The memories were too painful, the guilt still too strong.

The kettle whistled, startling her. She went through the motions of pouring the hot water over the tea bag, hoping the mundane chore would calm her. But her gaze kept darting back to the bracelet. She wondered where it had come from and where it had been all these years. She wondered about those dark stains.

Should she call Tom? He'd want to know about her latest discovery and yet she hesitated to reach out. She didn't want to worry him, but even more, she hated the notion of dragging Riley's sister back into this nightmare. The Cavanaughs had been through so much. Rae deserved a little peace. She and Tom deserved to be happy.

But was concern for her future sister-in-law the only reason for her hesitation? Maybe she didn't want to acknowledge even to herself that the bracelet might really be Riley's. Who besides the kidnapper could have had it all these years?

Despite her reservations, Ellie knew she needed to

tell someone. This wasn't the kind of discovery that could be swept under the rug. The bracelet could very well be evidence.

Plucking a baggie from underneath the sink, she carefully zipped the braid inside. The stains would need to be examined and tested, but nothing could be done at this late hour. Maybe she'd bypass her brother and go directly to Sam Reece. He had a broader reach and a lot more resources at his disposal. If nothing turned up in the tests, Rae would never have to know about the bracelet and Tom wouldn't be put in the uncomfortable and ill-advised position of keeping something from his fiancée.

So far nothing dangerous had happened to her, Ellie reasoned. The calls, the sightings and now the bracelet seemed dark and malicious, but she hadn't been physically threatened. Until that time, there was little her brother could do in an official capacity, and she certainly wasn't going to move into town with him and Rae. She wouldn't be chased from her home or her studio. She wouldn't have her life upended for…what? A prank? A hoax? Someone trying to get under her skin? If someone truly meant her harm, why broadcast his or her intentions?

Turning out the lights, she carried her tea upstairs, along with the bagged bracelet. Placing the cup on the nightstand, she went over to the dresser and opened the lid of her jewelry box. One of the trays concealed the compartment where she stored her most treasured keepsakes.

Removing her friendship bracelet from the box, she

placed it on the dresser and smoothed the braid with her fingertip. The blue yarn was unfaded, unstained and not frayed.

Pristine compared to the red bracelet.

SAM'S CELL PHONE woke him up. Usually a call came in the middle of the night when another child had gone missing and his team had been activated. Lately, however, he'd been hearing from Jenna Malloy at all hours. He braced himself as he fought his way up out of the haze.

He still wondered if he'd seen her on the street earlier. Wondered if she'd called from her own phone, pretending to be her roommate. He'd picked up on something in Hazel's voice that niggled. Maybe there was no Hazel Lamont. Why Jenna would pull such a childish prank, Sam had no idea, but he suspected she'd called at least once before pretending to be someone else. When he'd questioned the disguised voice, the caller had hung up and Jenna hadn't contacted him for months.

He lifted himself on his elbow and squinted at the clock he kept on his bedside table, along with his phone and watch. Overkill, he supposed, but old habits die hard. The digital display read a little past one o'clock. Approximately the same time Jenna had called the night before. However, when he picked up his cell phone, he was shocked to see Ellie Brannon's name on the screen.

He came wide-awake as he rolled over in bed and lifted the phone to his ear. "Agent Reece." She didn't say anything for so long that he wondered if his number had been called by mistake. "Hello?"

She cleared her throat. "It's Ellie Brannon."

"Is everything okay?" Sam asked.

Another pause. "I'm not sure. I'm fine physically. But something's happened."

He pushed himself up against the headboard. The illumination filtering in from the streetlights cast an eerie glow inside his bedroom. Fitting, he supposed, since Ellie Brannon's voice in his ear was like hearing from a ghost. "What's going on? Are you sure you're all right?"

"Yes, I'm fine." He heard her take a breath. "Look, this was a bad idea. An impulse. I'm sorry for disturbing you so late."

"Don't worry about that. You said something happened?"

"It's not an emergency. I can explain it all to you in the morning. Right now I should let you get back to sleep."

"No, don't hang up. Tell me what happened."

He put the phone on speaker, allowing her voice to fill his bedroom. Sam felt a shiver down his back as he swung his legs over the side of the bed and reached for his pants.

"When I came back from the studio tonight, I found a friendship bracelet looped over the handle of my back door," she said.

He stood and zipped up. "A friendship bracelet?"

"You've seen them. Yarn or embroidery floss braided together and tied around the wrist. A lot of kids used to wear them. They made a comeback when I was in middle school."

"I know the kind you mean. I remember my kid sister

and her friends wearing them." He picked up his watch from the nightstand and buckled it in place. "The bracelet obviously means something to you or you wouldn't have called. What's the significance?"

"Jenna, Riley and I made ours together. It was a huge production, picking out coordinating colors of yarn and so forth. Mine was blue, Jenna's yellow and Riley's red. But we each wove a strand of the other two colors in our braids to symbolize our friendship." She paused again. "I don't know if I'm explaining this well."

"No, I get the picture," Sam said. "Go on."

"The bracelet I found tonight is red. Like Riley's. With blue and yellow threads woven in."

"And you think the bracelet is hers?"

"I know that seems impossible. After all these years? After what she must have gone through?" He heard her take another breath and imagined her sitting in the dark, clutching the bracelet in her fist. Or maybe standing at the window, peering out at the moonlight. "Riley disappeared without a trace. Not so much as a scrap of torn clothing or a broken fingernail was found in the Ruins. Now fifteen years later her red friendship bracelet turns up at my back door. Except… I don't know if it's hers. I don't know what to think about any of the things that have happened recently."

He heard a tremor in her voice and took the phone off speaker. He wasn't sure why. The sound of her vulnerability in his quiet bedroom somehow seemed a little too intimate. He lifted the phone to his ear as he walked over to the window. "Tell me more about these bracelets."

"There's not a lot to tell. They've gone in and out of fashion over the years. When we were in middle school, everybody had one. They were cheap and easy to make. The one I found tonight looks old. It *could* be Riley's. The yarn is faded and frayed, and I noticed some dark stains that might be blood."

That got Sam's attention, though he tried to keep his voice neutral as he peered out into the night. "Maybe that's what someone wants you to think. Anyone could have made that bracelet and dirtied it up to make it look old."

"How would anyone know about those blue and yellow threads, though?"

"You said the three of you wore them in middle school. Someone could have noticed."

"And remembered all these years later? I don't think so. The threads are subtle."

"Where is the bracelet now?"

"Right here on the nightstand beside me. I put it in a plastic bag for safekeeping. If the stains are blood, you could order a DNA test and run the results through some kind of database, right? You could at least prove whether or not the DNA is Riley's."

"It's an interesting possibility." He tracked the headlights of a car pulling into the parking lot. Someone was out late. "Does Sheriff Brannon know about the bracelet?"

"No and I have my reasons for not calling him tonight. I would appreciate it if you wouldn't say anything until I have a chance to talk to him."

"Okay." Sam drawled the word as he considered this

turn of events. Curious that she would reach out to him instead of her brother. "I have to say, I'm surprised you decided to call me. You seemed reluctant to speak with me earlier."

"I know. I'm a little surprised myself," she admitted. "I suppose I owe you an explanation."

Sam's gaze was still on the car. The driver had killed the lights but no one got out. "You don't need to explain yourself to me," he said. "I'm just glad you told me about the bracelet."

"No, I think I need to get this out."

She seemed to want to talk and Sam was more than willing to listen. He closed his eyes briefly as her velvety voice seeped into him.

"Earlier after I found the bracelet, I sat for a while in the dark. The house was so quiet I could hear my own heartbeat. I kept thinking about Riley and Jenna… about the horrible things that were done to them. God, the images that went through my head…"

Sam knew all about those images.

"Most of the time, I try not to dwell on the past, but with everything that's happened recently… I don't know. I guess I just needed to hear a familiar voice. To connect with someone who understands what happened back then. Your number was on my nightstand so I called. I really am sorry for disturbing you so late."

Sam took a moment before he answered. He was a little more affected by her explanation than he wanted to admit. Images were also storming through his head. "I gave you my number so you could call whenever you needed to. The why doesn't matter."

"Doesn't it?"

"Only if you want it to." He squinted down at the parked car. He could see a silhouette behind the wheel. The driver was probably waiting for someone, but Sam's job had made him perpetually wary. It was too dark to see a license plate number. He committed a description of the vehicle to memory just in case. "I'm a little concerned about your brother, though. I'd hate to get off on the wrong foot with Sheriff Brannon as I reboot my investigation and I can't imagine he'll be too thrilled with either one of us if we leave him out of the loop. I think you should let him know about the bracelet. He can be at your house in fifteen minutes. It'll take me two hours to drive down."

"You don't need to drive down here tonight." She sounded taken aback by the mere suggestion. "Anyway, you'd have to break every speed limit between here and Dallas to make it in two hours even at this time of night."

"Wouldn't be the first time," he said.

"No, please don't come. That's not why I called. The bracelet seemed like a significant development, and as I said earlier, your number was handy. There's no need to come down here in person. Not tonight."

"Where are you now?" he asked.

She sounded surprised by the question. "I'm upstairs in my bedroom."

"Is the house secure?"

"The doors are locked and the security lights are on. There's a pistol in my nightstand and I know how to use it."

"Good."

"I'm not afraid, Agent Reece."

"It doesn't hurt to be a little afraid," he said. "Let's talk this through for a minute. You say Riley had on the bracelet the night she disappeared?"

"Yes. We teased her about it, but she didn't care. She was always good-natured about our ribbing. That night, though…"

"What about it?"

A long pause on Ellie's end. "She didn't want to go to the Ruins. She said she had a bad feeling about that place. I thought she was just scared by all the stories we'd heard, but looking back, it was almost as if she had some kind of premonition."

"Do you believe in premonitions?"

"I believe we all have internal warning systems and I believe those instincts are more finely tuned in some than in others. Riley felt strongly enough about the Ruins that she wore something that night she thought would protect her."

Sam leaned a shoulder against the window frame. His gaze remained fixed on the parked car. "Let's go back over that night. Everything you said, everything you did. The preparations you made before going out to the Ruins. Tell me anything at all that you can remember."

The old defensiveness crept back in. "I told you everything I remembered fifteen years ago. It's all in the files."

"Then tell me about Riley and Jenna. What were they like back then?"

She didn't say anything for the longest time and Sam thought at first she might not answer. Then he heard a soft sigh. "We were as close as sisters. We even looked alike. Same hair color, same size. Jenna was the smart one. Always so driven and intense, whether it was grades or sports or whatever. I wish you could have known her back then, Agent Reece. We all thought she would one day conquer the world. I've often wondered what she would have done with her life…the things she might have accomplished if I'd been taken instead of her."

"What about Riley?" Sam asked softly.

"She was the sweet one. Always smiling. Always so upbeat and warm. People naturally gravitated to her, but she didn't care about being popular. She came from money, but she was down-to-earth and humble. Everyone who knew her loved her."

"And you?"

She fell silent again. Sam watched the car below as he waited.

"As hard as it is to admit, there was a time when I cared too much about being popular."

"There's no shame in that," he said. "Teenagers are by nature shallow and self-centered."

"Oh, I was all that and more," she said with remorse. "Not that it's an excuse, but it wasn't always easy being the sheriff's kid. Just ask my brother. The other kids thought they had to watch their every move around us, especially in high school when our social lives became such a big deal. That was why I pushed Jenna and Riley to go out to the Ruins that night. Not just because we'd been dared, though that was important, too—it meant we'd been noticed. I wanted to prove that I wasn't above breaking a few rules now and then. If I'd been even slightly less selfish and immature, things would have turned out very differently that night."

"What happened wasn't your fault," Sam said.

"I know that rationally. But it doesn't change the fact that it was my idea to sneak out of the house and ride our bikes out to the lake. I knew Riley was afraid. I could have backed off at any time, but I just kept pushing and pushing until she finally gave in. Once we were inside, I had to prove how brave I was. That's how we got separated. I went upstairs and left Jenna and Riley alone."

"You had no way of knowing what would happen. If you'd stayed with them, you might have been taken, too."

"I don't think that's true. I was attacked when I came back downstairs. He must have already subdued Jenna and Riley. Drugged them, knocked them unconscious. I don't know how he did it. But I do know that if he'd wanted to take me, too, he would have."

"Why do you think you were left behind?" Sam asked.

"I've asked myself that question a thousand times. The only thing that makes any sense is that I was the sheriff's daughter. Ironic, isn't it, since that's the reason I went out to the Ruins in the first place."

"Who else knew you would be there that night?"

"It wasn't a secret. All our friends were aware that some of the older kids had dared us."

"Anyone specific dare you?"

He heard a shrug in her voice. "Word got around. That's the way it worked back then. Someone told someone who told someone else who told us. But you already know all this. You asked these same questions fifteen years ago. I don't know what good it does to go through it again."

"You've refreshed my memory on some of the details," Sam said. "That's always helpful."

"I guess. But I think I've done enough talking for one night. It's late and you probably have to be at work in a few hours."

"I don't require much sleep." He turned away from the window, reluctant to let Ellie hang up.

"Why do you think all this is happening?" she asked. "What do you really think is going on?"

Now it was Sam who paused. "I don't know. But I promise you one thing. I'm going to find out."

"It's never a good idea to make promises you can't keep, Agent Reece."

Chapter Seven

Ellie was startled to find Sam sitting on her deck steps the next morning when she came downstairs. Despite their late-night phone conversation, she'd risen at her usual time, showered, dressed and dried her hair. Adhering to a routine gave her the illusion of being in control, but the startled thump of her heart at the sight of the FBI agent disabused her of that notion.

She paused at the kitchen window to study his silhouette. He had a strong profile, though his nose was slightly crooked. She wondered if he'd been injured in the line of duty. She didn't recall any physical imperfections from fifteen years ago. She only remembered how intimidated she'd been by the abrasive federal agent who had interviewed her. Intimidated and in awe, if she were truthful. If the circumstances had been different, she might have developed a crush on Agent Reece, but she would never have admitted it in a million years. Instead, she'd cultivated an intense dislike and distrust of the man for pushing her to remember details of a night she desperately wanted to forget. He'd seemed so much older than her back then, more worldly and sophisticated, but here they were fifteen years later, both in their thirties and both looking for answers. Funny how time had a way of narrowing divides.

He sat in the shade but a tiny shaft of sunlight filtered down through the leaves, shimmering off the silver that was nearly invisible at his temples. He was dressed in his usual attire of suit trousers and dress shirt. Leaving his coat and tie in the car was undoubtedly his idea of dressing down. Ellie wondered if he even owned a pair of jeans, much less a T-shirt and sneakers. His adherence to a strict dress code once again gave her second thoughts about her shorts and sandals, but then she shrugged. She lived and worked in the boonies. No reason to dress up for Agent Reece or anyone else. She was who she was.

Instead of going outside to join him right away, she toasted bagels while the coffee brewed and then assembled cups on a tray, along with cream cheese, jam and fresh fruit. He rose when he heard the back door and strode over to offer his assistance.

"Good morning, Agent Reece," she greeted. "You do know you're trespassing on private property, don't you?"

"I would have knocked, but I thought you might be sleeping in this morning. I didn't think you'd mind if I waited." He nodded toward the loaded tray. "That's quite a spread. I hope you didn't go to all that trouble on my account."

"I didn't," Ellie replied bluntly. "I always have breakfast on the deck when the weather is nice." His unwavering regard disconcerted her, and she avoided his gaze as she set the table and poured the coffee. "What are you doing here so early, anyway? You must have left Dallas at the crack of dawn."

"I wanted to beat the traffic."

"Well, as long as you're here, you may as well sit and have a bite to eat." She waved him to a chair and handed him a cup of coffee.

"Thank you." He accepted the coffee with gratitude, but waited until she sat before taking his place across from her. "This is a real treat. I usually grab something on the run."

"It's just bagels and fruit. Took all of five minutes to put together." She sounded defensive and made an effort to soften her tone. Giving him a quick smile, she unfolded her napkin and tried to act normal. She didn't want to contemplate why she felt so nervous in Agent Reece's company. Yesterday she'd been defensive because of their past and because she'd been certain he still thought she was hiding something. This was a different kind of tension. In the space of one phone call, something had changed between them and she didn't know why.

Or maybe she did. It was simple, really. She'd let down her guard with Sam Reece. She'd allowed him a glimpse of her vulnerability and now the familiarity between them made her uncomfortable. Strange that the more awkward she became in his presence, the more at ease he seemed, as if he found it perfectly natural to be seated across from her at the breakfast table. Maybe he was used to sharing meals, but Ellie was a loner and had always told herself she preferred it that way.

He eyed her over the rim of his cup. "Everything okay this morning? You seem a little subdued. No more discoveries or phone calls?"

"I've got a lot on my mind these days. But no, nothing since the bracelet." She scooted back her chair. "Should I go get it for you? I assume that's why you're here."

"No hurry. Finish your breakfast."

She nodded reluctantly and settled back down. "What will you do with it? What's the protocol?"

"I'll log it into evidence and send it to the lab for analysis. I have to warn you, these things take time. A case this old won't be considered a priority. It could take weeks to get back the results."

"You can't call in a favor to speed things up?" she asked hopefully. Their gazes connected for a moment before she glanced away.

"I'll do what I can."

She picked up her cup and then set it back down. "This is awkward. I feel I need to clear the air before we go any further."

"About?"

"I want to apologize again for calling you in the middle of the night. I don't know what I was thinking."

"I told you, I gave you my number for precisely that reason. You did the right thing."

He spoke so matter-of-factly Ellie found herself relaxing, but she didn't know if that was a good thing or not. She wanted to believe Agent Reece's charm and goodwill were genuine, but he seemed so different from the intense young agent she remembered. Had he really changed that much or was he playing her? If so, to what end?

"What is it?" he asked.

"I'm sorry?" she asked in confusion.

"You were staring at me now with a pained look on your face." He put down his cup and returned her stare across the table. "I get it. You still don't trust me. But you can. I'm not your enemy."

"There was a time when it seemed like you were my enemy."

"For that, *I* apologize. I had a lot to learn back in those days. But my only objective then and now is to find out what happened to Riley. If possible, to bring her kidnapper to justice. I could still use your help."

She drew a deep breath and slowly released it as if she could somehow let go of the past. Something came to her as the morning breeze drifted across her deck. Fifteen years ago, Agent Reece had conducted himself poorly in his zeal to uncover the truth, but Ellie had clung to her resentment mostly out of fear. Fear that he might be right about her buried memories. What if she had glimpsed the kidnapper's face that night? What if she could have identified him years ago if only she'd had the courage to explore her subconscious?

"I can't be hypnotized," she blurted.

A brow rose at her adamant tone, but his voice remained calmly encouraging. "I'm not talking about hypnosis. I need you to stay alert. Make sure you keep the doors locked and your guard up. Call me if you see or hear anything the slightest bit suspicious. Night or day. I mean that."

Her gaze burned into his. "What else?"

He waited a long beat before he answered. "Return to the scene of the crime with me."

Her heart skipped a beat at the prospect. "Go out to the Ruins, you mean? Do you know what you're asking of me?"

"It's been fifteen years. Don't you think it's time you went back?"

"I've been back."

He cocked his head slightly. "When?"

"A few years ago. I got as far as the doorway."

"You didn't go inside?"

"I couldn't." A panic attack had frozen her at the doorway. She likened the episode to being trapped in her worst nightmare for what had seemed an eternity. When the paralysis finally subsided, she'd turned and headed for home as fast as she could run and hadn't dared go back.

"I think you should try again," he said.

"Easy for you to say."

His voice softened. "There's nothing to be afraid of. I'll be with you every step of the way."

That note in his voice…the way he looked at her…

She had *everything* to be afraid of.

Ellie lifted her gaze. "Surely you don't mean right now. Today."

He sat back in his chair, his posture loose, but his gaze still deeply intense. "We should wait until dark. If we're going to retrace your steps, I'd like to see everything the way you saw it."

She couldn't seem to get rid of the icy needles at the

base of her spine. "I'm on the air tonight until midnight. It was just after ten when we went out there that night. Besides, you can't recreate something that happened fifteen years ago. The landscape has changed and there isn't a blood moon."

"Then we'll have to make do with ordinary moonlight. I don't expect you to decide right now. Just give it some thought. I plan to be in town for a couple of days. Maybe we can set something up for tomorrow night. You're off the air on weekends, right?"

"Yes." She told herself not to give him a definitive answer. She needed time to think this through. But what if a trip to the Ruins could trigger a memory? What if returning to the scene of the crime could help lay old ghosts to rest? She wouldn't be alone. Sam would be with her every step of the way. Even so, her pulse quickened as she closed her eyes and saw herself standing in the arched doorway, peering through layers of cobwebs and shadows in search of the monster that lay hidden in her memories.

She turned to the lake, sweeping her gaze over the shimmering water. If she went down to the dock, she'd be able to see the smokestack of the old boiler room rising up through the pine trees.

"You okay?"

The deep timber of his voice drew her back to the deck. Ellie stood abruptly and began clearing the table. "I'll think about it and let you know. Right now, though, I have a lot of work to do to prepare for tonight's show. Books to skim, blogs to read..."

He reached over and put his hand over hers to still her. “If you could spare another minute…”

A tremor shot through her. She pulled her hand away and sat back down. “What is it?”

“You mentioned a reporter named Melanie Kent yesterday. I told you I would look into her.”

Ellie said anxiously, “What did you find out?”

“Your brother was right about her employment history. She’s lost several positions in the past five years and is apparently in between jobs at the moment. You were also right about her aspirations. It seems she’s writing another book.”

“How do you know that?”

“I’ve scanned her blog and social media accounts.”

Ellie sat forward. “She has a blog?”

“I’ll text you a link. She writes mainly about cold cases in the tristate area. That seems to be her area of interest.”

“That doesn’t surprise me. I met her years after Riley’s kidnapping and she was still obsessed with the case.”

“Her obsession doesn’t appear to have abated,” Sam said. “She has a lot of material on her blog about the investigation—inside stuff. At one time, she must have had sources within the Nance County sheriff’s office.”

Ellie nodded. “My dad worried about that. Some of the information that turned up in the papers could only have come from inside his department, but he could never root out the leaker.” She paused. “This new book she’s writing. Is it about the kidnapping?”

“Apparently, it deals more with the aftermath. The

time frame is a week or two after the kidnapping until present day. It seems she's working on a whatever-happened-to angle." He searched her face as if anticipating her reaction. "She's calling it *The Girl That Got Away*."

A thrill shot down Ellie's spine. "Meaning Jenna or me?"

"Could be both, I guess."

"The caller told me the other night that Preacher is coming for me because I'm the one that got away. Now Melanie Kent is back in Belle Pointe and all these weird things start happening. This can't be a coincidence."

"I'm inclined to agree, but I don't want to jump to any conclusions until I've had a chance to talk with her."

"You haven't been able to find her, either?"

"She gave up her apartment in Dallas a few weeks ago and didn't leave a forwarding address. She isn't registered at any of the area hotels and motels as far as I can determine."

"She's been known to use an alias," Ellie said. "Try Marie Nightingale."

Sam's gaze turned curious. "I'm guessing there's a story behind that name."

"When she was writing her first book, she called a few times under her real name trying to get an interview with me. I wouldn't agree to talk to her so she started calling into the college radio show I hosted using the alias Marie Nightingale. She pretended to be the survivor of a brutal kidnapping. Each time she called, she recounted the most harrowing and horrifying details about her time in captivity."

"Given your background, you were naturally sympathetic to her story," Sam said.

"I hung on her every word and so did my listeners. She was that good. After we'd established a rapport, she asked to meet for coffee and I agreed. I knew it wasn't a good idea, but I felt sorry for her and she was an expert at using my survivor's guilt against me. I couldn't help Riley, but maybe I could somehow help Marie."

"What happened?"

"The next thing I knew she'd wormed her way into every aspect of my life, trolling for dirt to include in her book. One of my friends became alarmed by her obsessive behavior. She told my brother about Marie and he dug around until he uncovered her real identity."

"You haven't had any contact with her since then?"

"Right after the book came out, I took a couple of calls on my show from someone pretending to be a fan. She asked a lot of probing questions and I wondered at the time if the caller might be Marie… Melanie."

"You didn't recognize her voice?"

Ellie met his dark gaze and shivered. "Like I said, she was that good."

AFTER LEAVING ELLIE'S place that morning, Sam made the two-and-a-half-hour drive back to Dallas to fill out the necessary paperwork that would accompany the friendship bracelet to the crime lab in Virginia. He made a few phone calls, hoping to rush things along, but he doubted even under the best of circumstances that he'd hear anything for a few weeks. He worked at his desk until after lunch and then by late afternoon, he was back in Nance County. Instead of driving to the lake or into Belle Pointe, he took the scenic route out to Cory Small's farm.

The lush countryside hadn't changed much in fifteen years. The paved road was shaded by a deep pine forest and scented with honeysuckle that grew in thick hedges along the ditches. Sam lowered his window, letting the fragrant country air wash through his car.

He knew the way despite the passage of time. After the local authorities had requested FBI assistance, Sam had driven out a couple of times with the first Sheriff Brannon and once by himself to talk to Silas Creed's sister. He remembered Ellen Small as a thin, harried woman with a sad smile and a careworn expression. The son, Cory, had been a senior in high school at the time of the kidnapping. Both Sam and Sheriff Brannon had taken a hard look at the boy, but he'd had an alibi for the night in question and nothing so much as a speeding ticket on his record. By all accounts, he was a good kid and model student, courteous, cooperative and protective of his mother.

As Sam neared his destination, professionally painted signs advertising the farm cropped up on the side of the road. He'd done a little research before leaving Dallas. Cory Small had expanded the business after his mother died, adding a nursery and landscaping service to the vegetable gardens. The farm also offered hayrides, picnics and seasonal berry picking to elementary schools in the area. If parents and school officials remembered Cory Small's relationship to Silas Creed, they didn't seem to hold it against him.

A young woman wearing a green logo T-shirt waved from behind one of the fresh produce stands as he turned off the main road. The gates were still open so he drove right through, his tires crunching on loose gravel as he pulled into the parking lot.

He got out and glanced around at his surroundings. The property was beautifully landscaped with lush shrubs and trees and wooden tubs overflowing with flowers. Sam adjusted his tie and put on his suit coat despite the heat. People tended to respond more cooperatively to a professional presentation.

A man watering the hanging baskets gave him a brief nod as he took in the business attire.

"Can I help you?"

"I'm looking for Cory Small."

"He was in the greenhouse last I saw him. Straight back. You can't miss it."

"Thanks."

Sam made his way through the maze of plant beds and displays of ceramic planters toward the greenhouse. The doors were open and two women milled about inside, admiring the orchids. Sam spotted a man at the back unloading more plants. He was in his early thirties, average height, lean build, deeply tanned. He smiled and nodded pleasantly as Sam approached.

"I'm looking for Cory Small," Sam said. "I was told I could find him in the greenhouse."

"And so you have. What can I do for you today? If you're looking for an orchid, the cymbidiums just arrived this morning. They're about as fresh as you can get in these parts. We also have a few exotics, but they'll cost you," he warned.

"I'm not here to buy a plant." Sam took out his credentials. "Agent Sam Reece with the FBI. Do you have a moment to talk?"

The man's guard went up. The smile disappeared as he straightened, casting a wary glance toward the entrance where customers still lingered over the orchids. Then he scanned Sam's identification and glanced up with a frown. "Don't I know you? Yeah, I remember you now. You and Sheriff Brannon came out here to talk to my mother about my uncle after those girls disappeared. You came back the next day by yourself. You asked a lot of questions, as I recall. What's this about, anyway?" His voice dropped as he tugged off his work gloves. "Have you found my uncle?"

"Silas Creed remains a person of interest and is still at large so far as we know. But there has been a new development in the case," Sam said.

The man's expression grew even more guarded. "What would that be?"

"I'm not at liberty to say. Is there somewhere more private where we can speak?"

Cory Small looked as if he wanted to refuse, but then nodded and motioned for Sam to follow him out the back door of the greenhouse. Sam paused as his gaze lit on a black hat hanging from a wooden peg inside the door.

"Is that your hat?" he asked.

Cory glanced back, startled. "I'm sorry, what?" His gaze went to the wall and he frowned. "Oh, the hat. It was my mother's. I can't remember a time she didn't have that thing on when she was working out in the sun. I keep it around because she's still so much a part of this place." He paused reverently. "I've kept all her favorite tools, too. Didn't seem right to get rid of them." He nodded to the crowded pegs beside the hat.

Sam took in the memorial as he expressed his condolences. Silas Creed had been depicted with a similar hat on the ceiling of the Ruins. Sam thought about the description Ellie had given of the person she'd seen the day before—average height, slim build. Wide-brim hat pulled down low to hide his features. His gaze went back to Cory Small.

"She's been gone nearly five years and I still miss her every day," he said. "Always will, I guess."

"It's hard losing a parent no matter your age."

Cory nodded. "My mother's life wasn't easy. I comfort myself that she's at peace now."

He stared at the hat for a moment longer, still with a contemplative frown, before he turned to the back exit and stepped outside. Sam followed him out. They walked several yards away from the greenhouse before Cory turned. "Why don't you tell me the real reason you're here, Agent Reece? If you haven't found my uncle, what is it you want to talk to me about?"

"As I said, there's been a new development. Since the case has never been closed, we follow up on every lead."

Cory ran fingers through his hair as he glanced out over his property. "I'd like to help you. I really would. But I don't know what more I can do. My mother and

I told you everything we could about my uncle after he left town."

"A lot can happen in fifteen years," Sam said. "You or your mother never had any contact with Silas Creed after he disappeared? No phone calls or letters?"

A shadow drifted over the man's features. Something that might have been anger glinted in his eyes. "All these years later and you people are still trying to drag her into that nightmare."

"I don't mean any disrespect," Sam said. "I'm just trying to get at the facts."

"The facts? How many times do we have to tell you? We never saw or heard from my uncle after that night nor did we help him leave town. If you want to know the truth, we were both glad he was gone. We felt terrible about what happened to those girls—"

"Riley Cavanaugh and Jenna Malloy," Sam supplied.

The shadow deepened. "Yes. Riley and Jenna. I went to school with them. My mother knew their families. We would have done anything to change what happened. You can't imagine what it was like for her, knowing her brother had done such a terrible thing. It took years off her life. So, no. I wouldn't have lifted a finger to help him."

"But you can understand why we'd wonder if you had," Sam said. "It's not easy to disappear without a trace."

"That may be true, but my uncle was a lot more resourceful than most people gave him credit for. He was smart and educated. Brilliant in some ways. Read everything he could get his hands on. Highly functional when he took his meds."

"And when he didn't take his medication?"

Cory winced. "He could be volatile. At times, violent. Which was why my mother didn't want him living under the same roof with us. I think her childhood must have been pretty traumatic before her parents sent him away. The stories I've heard?" He shook his head. "After the hospital closed down and they turned out all the patients, she got him a place in town, helped him find work. Saw to it that he had enough money for food and bills. She did what she could and hoped for the best. Then all those stories started getting back to her about how he would stare in people's windows at night and how he would sometimes stand outside the fence at the elementary school, watching the children play. I don't know if any of that was true. You know how cruel people can be, especially when someone is different. But the locals didn't like having him around and that wore on my mother."

"Was he ever violent with either of you?" Sam asked.

"He never hit us or anything, but he could be scary as all get out when he lost control. He'd get this look in his eyes? I remember once when I was about twelve or thirteen, he tried to chop down our front door with an ax. My mother and I hid in a closet until Sheriff Brannon arrived. Who knows what would have happened if he'd gotten inside? I kept my distance after that night."

"How do you suppose he was able to take Riley and Jenna from the Ruins all by himself without any signs of a struggle? He wasn't a big man and yet somehow he subdued three teenage girls and knocked Tom Brannon out cold."

Cory nodded. "I've thought about that. He wasn't big but he was tough as nails. All that physical labor kept him in shape. He had a truck, too, don't forget. He could have loaded those girls in the back and driven across the state line before anyone knew they were missing."

"And then he drove Jenna back to the area nearly three weeks later and let her go?"

"You're the FBI agent. You tell me how he did it."

"It's possible he had help," Sam said. "It's also possible Jenna and Riley were held somewhere nearby. This area is rural with dozens of abandoned farmhouses and barns, not to mention basements and storm cellars. We're talking miles and miles of dense forest. No way to cover every inch of it."

"Yes, but if they were still in the area, wouldn't the bloodhounds have picked up the trail?"

"If your uncle was as smart as you say, he would have known how to mask their scent. But that's a lot for one person to accomplish in a short amount of time. Did your uncle have any close friends or buddies?"

"Buddies? Are you serious?"

"You never saw him hanging out with anyone?"

"People around here thought my uncle a weirdo at best and a psycho at worst. I guess they were right on both counts."

"He was able to get work so he must have had some interaction with the locals."

"People gave him work as a favor to my mother." Cory shoved his hands in his pockets and glanced back at the greenhouse. "Look, this is just a rehash of what we discussed fifteen years ago. I don't have anything new to add to the conversation so if you'll excuse me, I really need to get back to work."

"Just a couple more questions," Sam said. "You mentioned stories about your uncle that got back to your mother. Is that the reason she brought him to the farm to live?"

"She didn't exactly bring him here to live. Sometimes he just needed a place to crash when he took a bad turn. She'd let him stay in the garden shed at the back of the property until things leveled out. He had a kitchenette he could use, a bathroom with a shower, everything he needed, and she made sure he had a warm bed and plenty to eat. He'd sometimes spend weeks holed up out there and never talk to another living soul except for my mother. When he got better, he'd go back to his place in town."

"Is the garden shed still standing?" Sam asked.

"Yeah, it's in pretty good shape. I recently repaired the roof and added a fresh coat of paint. Sometimes one of my seasonal workers needs a place to stay so I try to keep the place livable."

"Is anyone staying there now? I'd like to take a look around before I leave."

Cory frowned. "Why? If you didn't find anything out there fifteen years ago, what makes you think you'll find something now?"

"I don't expect to find anything. Like I said, I just want to take a look around." Sam gave him a pointed look. "Is there a reason you don't want me to go out there?"

He shrugged. "Normally, no, but I've got the place rented out. I don't let strangers stay there as a rule but she was pretty persuasive. One of the stipulations of our agreement is that she be allowed to work without interruption."

"She?"

"Someone from the city. A writer named Melanie Kent."

Chapter Eight

Sam glanced over his shoulder as he strode along the dirt path. Cory Small had returned to the greenhouse and Sam didn't see anyone else about. He'd pretended to go back to his car after their talk, but instead had doubled back once Cory was out of sight.

No wonder he and Tom Brannon had had so much difficulty locating Melanie Kent. The reporter had purposefully dropped off the grid while she wrote another book about the kidnapping. What better inspiration than Silas Creed's former retreat, the place where he'd been holed up when he abducted Jenna and Riley and left Ellie and her brother for dead?

As the structure came into view, Sam paused once more to search his surroundings. Nestled at the tree line, the garden-shed-turned-cottage was quiet and secluded. The charcoal color blended with the deep shade of the woods. Two small windows flanked the entrance and a metal awning over the front door provided protection from inclement weather.

Sam could almost imagine Silas Creed peering out one of the windows, tracking his approach. The hair lifted at the back of his nape. He didn't believe in ghosts or demons, but in his experience, evil had a tendency to linger in physical places. He tried to shake off a dark foreboding as he walked the perimeter, noting the placement of windows and the rear exit before he came back around to knock. He rapped firmly and the door creaked open. Melanie Kent hadn't felt the need to lock up, which likely meant she was either inside or somewhere nearby. He toed the crack wider.

"Federal Agent! I'm here to see Melanie Kent. Anyone home?"

He glanced over his shoulder. The path behind him remained clear. He turned back to the door and called out again. "This is Agent Sam Reece with the FBI. I need to speak with Melanie Kent."

Still no response.

He pushed the door inward and stepped over the threshold. The late afternoon sun shone through the open windows, creating shafts of warm light in the shadowy interior. His gaze swept the room. No red glowing eyes peering around furniture. No lurking silhouettes in darkened doorways.

No Melanie Kent, either.

On first glance, the place seemed almost pleasant in its utilitarian design. The rough-hewn walls had been painted white, but the floor and ceiling beams had been left natural. It was only on deeper scrutiny that one noticed the gloom creeping in from the corners.

Sam took a moment to scope out the place. The kitchenette was located to his immediate left and the living space to his right consisted of a worn chair, a neatly made daybed and a small desk, which doubled as a nightstand. A ceiling fan stirred pages in a yellow legal pad that had been tossed on the bed and the dozens of images that had been tacked to the wall above the desk.

Sam took a quick glance out one of the front windows before he strode across the room to browse the photographs. Melanie Kent had divided the images into two categories—people and places. Sam started with the Ruins. The reporter had shot the crumbling hospital from every angle at various times of the day. The place looked to be in a lot worse shape than he remembered. Most of the front windows were broken and boarded and the roof had collapsed in places. An old wheelchair lay upended in the weeds. Sam studied the exterior shots before following the photographic trail inside where graffiti covered the walls and Preacher peered down from the ceiling. The red glowing eyes beneath the brim of the black hat seemed to pierce right through the camera lens.

Upstairs, the reporter had meticulously documented the shadowy rooms where gurneys and rat-infested mattresses had been piled to the ceiling, and on the third floor, where sunlight glimmered down through the holes in the roof and vines snaked in through jagged windows.

She'd photographed the lake, the Cavanaugh ranch and various locations in Belle Pointe, including the sheriff's office and the houses where Jenna Malloy and Ellie Brannon had grown up.

Then there were the people pictures—old photographs of Ellie, Riley and Jenna intermixed with recent snapshots of Jenna and Ellie. Neither woman appeared to know she was being surveilled, much less photographed. Melanie had taken only a few candid shots of Jenna, but dozens of Ellie relaxing on her deck, exiting her studio and standing on the dock, peering down into the water. Apparently she'd been watching Ellie for weeks. Sam took his time with those images, but eventually his attention drifted back to Jenna.

He removed one of the photographs for a closer scrutiny. Jenna was sitting on the porch steps of a white house—presumably her place in Dallas—gazing out at the street. It was an arresting shot, quiet and pensive, and yet Sam found something unsettling about her facial expression and body language.

His pulse jumped as he plucked one of the older photographs of Riley from the wall, his focus going back and forth between the photographs. The same tilt of the head, the same dreamy half smile…

Why would Jenna emulate Riley's mannerisms so closely? Or had it been the other way around?

He moved over to the window to examine the photographs in better lighting. The similarities to Riley were troubling enough, but now he saw something in the shot of Jenna that he hadn't noticed before.

A woman stood at a window peering out at Jenna. The porch lay in deep shadows, rendering the silhouette nearly invisible. Sam wondered if Melanie Kent even realized she'd captured a second person in the photo. Who might this mystery person be? Hazel Lamont, perhaps? Maybe Jenna's new roommate existed, after all.

He told himself there was nothing strange or unusual

about someone gazing out a window. Yet his uneasiness deepened as he remembered his conversation with the roommate and his initial impression that he might have been speaking to Jenna. Had Hazel Lamont deliberately manipulated him into doubting her identity?

Taking out his phone, he clicked off a few frames and returned the photographs to the wall. Then he picked up the legal pad and thumbed through the handwritten draft, pausing here and there to skim a passage.

The girls were similar in appearance—indeed, they were often mistaken for sisters—but as different as night and day in personality and upbringing.

Riley came from money. That alone set her apart. Before the start of each school year, her sister, Rae, would plan a weekend excursion to Dallas for the two of them. Booking a suite at the Ritz, they'd pamper themselves with expensive lunches, spa treatments and lavish shopping sprees.

Her two best friends could hardly imagine such luxury, though Jenna's family was comfortably middle class and she was a coddled only child. The Malloys lived in a beautifully restored Victorian house on King Street with lush front and back gardens and a maid who came every two weeks to clean the house and do the laundry. Independent and assertive, Jenna was the first of the trio to go away to summer camp, the first to get her own cell phone and later, the first to earn her learner's permit.

Ellie Brannon's family lived in a modest two-story home on Oak Street. Her father was the county sheriff and her mother a homemaker who sometimes worked as a substitute teacher to bring in extra income. From an early age, the kids were expected to pull their weight. Ellie babysat to earn spending money and her brother, Tom, mowed lawns. Rather than extravagant shopping trips to Dallas for school clothes, Ellie had to settle for outlet malls and thrift stores. She once bought a pale blue cashmere sweater from a church rummage sale only to discover that it was one of Riley Cavanaugh's castaways. The humiliation dogged Ellie for months and fed into the jealousy that had already put a strain on the friendship.

Jealousy? That was the first Sam had heard of any trouble between Ellie and Riley. He took the revelation with a grain of salt. He'd learned the hard way that Melanie Kent relied heavily on artistic license to create drama.

Sam scanned a few more pages and then tossed the notebook back on the bed. Taking another quick glance around the room, he left through the same door he'd entered.

The sun had dipped beneath the treetops by this time, casting long shadows across the path. He stepped to the edge of the woods, keeping a sharp eye out as he checked his voice mail. He didn't have to wait long. A woman dressed in jeans, sneakers and a striped T-shirt came hurrying along the trail. Her sunglasses and the brim of her floppy hat disguised her features, but Sam had no doubt as to *her* identity. Who else but Melanie Kent would be headed for the garden shed at this time of day?

Using bushes for concealment, he pressed deeper

into the shadows as someone called out her name. She glanced over her shoulder and then turned as Cory Small came into view. Removing her sunglasses, she dropped them into the tote slung over her shoulder and moved beneath the awning to wait.

"I'm in a hurry," she said as he approached. "Whatever this is about, can it wait?"

"No, it can't," he said bluntly. "You've been dodging me for days and I'm sick and tired of your runaround. We agreed on a weekly rental, remember? That means you pay up every Friday, but I haven't seen a dime since you moved in."

She folded her arms. "We also agreed I wouldn't be disturbed while I work, but here you are."

His voice hardened. "You're giving *me* attitude? Get over yourself. I'm not running a charity here. I only agreed to let you use this place because I needed the extra cash."

She gestured toward the nursery and gardens in the background. "Looks like you're doing all right to me."

"This is a slow time of year so I need every buck I can get my hands on just to make payroll. If you can't afford to pay what you owe, then pack up and get out."

"Or what? You'll throw me out? I told you I'd have your money by the weekend and I will so ease up, Bubba."

He caught her by the arm. "Don't call me that."

"Let go of me," she said in a deadly quiet voice.

"You think you can just blow me off? This is still my property."

"I *said* let go of me." She yanked her arm free, but they still stood toe to toe, face-to-face.

For a moment, Sam thought he might have to step out of his hiding place and intervene. This was a side of Cory Small he'd never witnessed before.

"Careful," Melanie taunted. "You just might reveal your true colors."

"What's that supposed to mean?"

She threw her head back. "I know your type. Good ol' boy on the surface with all kinds of nasty resentment festering beneath."

"You don't know anything about me."

"I know *everything* about you. I've researched every aspect of your uncle's life and how closely it intersected with yours and your mother's. I even found out something the cops don't know."

Sam stood stone still, riveted by the argument as he peered through the leaves.

"Oh, yeah? Like what?" Cory demanded.

"You'll have to read my book to find out."

He gave a derisive snort. "That's what I thought. You don't know anything."

"I guess we'll see, won't we?"

He seemed amused now. He folded his arms and leaned a shoulder against the wall. "Instead of keeping all these little secrets to yourself, maybe you should talk to the FBI agent that came by a little while ago. He sure seemed interested in you. He even wanted to come out here and take a look around."

Melanie stared at him for a moment. Then she glanced down the trail uneasily as she clutched the strap of her tote. "What FBI agent? You better not be lying to me."

"Now, why would I lie to you?" Cory drawled. "Fiction is your specialty, not mine."

"I don't write fiction."

"That's your opinion."

Sam saw her draw a deep breath, as if she were hanging onto her temper by a thread.

"Did you get his name?" she asked.

"Agent Sam Reece. He's not exactly a stranger in these parts."

"I know who he is. Did he say what he wanted?"

"What's it worth to you?"

"For God's sakes, just tell me!"

Cory looked as if he were thoroughly enjoying himself now that he thought he had the upper hand. "Maybe I'll write a book so you can find out."

"Don't be an ass. Tell me what he said."

"Apparently, there's been a new development in the Riley Cavanaugh case. He was pretty tight-lipped, but I'm starting to wonder if it has something to do with you. Strange how you turned up out of the blue the way you did."

"What's so strange about it?"

"You're up to something. I can feel it."

"I'm writing a book, moron. That's what I'm up to."

He let the insult roll off his back this time, but Sam saw the glitter of something unpleasant in the man's eyes. "Moron, huh? I'm smart enough to recognize bad news when I see it. See, I know you took something from the greenhouse the other night. I just can't figure out why."

"What are you talking about?"

"My mother's hat. The one that hangs on the wall? It was missing when I went to lock up night before last. Today it was back in its normal place."

She shrugged. "Maybe one of your workers borrowed it."

"They know better. Taking something without asking permission seems more like something you'd do."

"I have my own hat, thank you. I wouldn't dream of desecrating that little shrine you've erected to your mother. But keep telling yourself Agent Reece was here because of me. Denial is not just a river as they say."

"You really are a smug little—"

"Watch it, Bubba. Your misogyny is showing."

As Sam exited the nursery, he noticed a beige sedan parked in the shade of a large oak tree. The sun glinted off the windshield so that he could make out little more than a female silhouette behind the wheel. She ducked her head when she saw him staring. Then she started the engine and peeled out, showering gravel in her wake.

Sam wondered if the vehicle was the same one he'd seen the night before outside his townhome in Dallas. He had a dark hunch that Hazel Lamont was the driver. He hadn't been sure she existed until now, but the snapshot he'd found in the garden shed had convinced him otherwise. There was something intriguing about that figure at the window. Something a little disturbing about the way she watched Jenna from behind the glass. Sam got out his phone and enlarged the image. The shadows hid her features, but he had the impression of malice. His imagination or gut instinct?

Sam pocketed his phone and strode to his car. He had no idea why Jenna Malloy's roommate would be following him, but he intended to find out.

He left the farm and headed toward Belle Pointe. The road behind him remained clear until he reached the city limits and then he caught a glimpse of the beige sedan in his rearview mirror. He slowed and the vehicle quickly gained on him until the driver seemed to realize her mistake and backed off the gas. Sam drove through town, stopping for every yellow light to allow his pursuer time to catch up.

He pulled into the Belle Pointe Inn, removed his bag and checked in. Then he rode the elevator up to his third-floor room and after a quick perusal of his accommodations, he went over to the window and parted the curtains. The beige sedan was parked across the street facing the inn.

Sam strode out of the room and took the stairs two at a time down to the lobby. By the time he exited the building, the vehicle had disappeared.

ELLIE WAITED UNTIL she was safely home that night to check her messages. Sam had left a voice mail just after nine o'clock when her broadcast had barely begun. Maybe he'd lost track of the time or had forgotten when her program started. Or maybe his message was so important that he hadn't wanted to wait until she was off the air, much less until morning. However, he didn't sound urgent nor did he give her a clue as to why he was calling. He merely asked that she return his call when she got the chance.

Ellie tapped her fingers against the counter in deep contemplation. Maybe the reason for the call was to try to arrange a time for a trip to the Ruins. In which case, she needn't call back until morning because she hadn't yet made up her mind. Retracing her steps on the night of the kidnapping might seem a reasonable thing to do, but the very thought filled her with dread. She'd visited that place too many times in her nightmares. If she closed her eyes, she could imagine a dark-clad figure in a parson's hat skulking through the shadowy corridors, waiting until she had her back turned to grab her.

She'd researched the effects of chloroform, knew that even with a saturated rag pressed to the nose and mouth, it could take five minutes or longer to subdue a victim. Yet she couldn't remember much of a struggle. Surely she'd fought her assailant until she'd succumbed to the fumes, but all she remembered was a hand clamped to her mouth and then darkness. Had she glimpsed the kidnapper's face before she'd gone under?

How could a single attacker overcome three teenage girls without one of them managing to break free? Maybe someone really had helped Silas Creed that night and now the accomplice had once again turned his attention to the girl that got away.

Ellie replayed Sam's message. His tone was calm and measured. Almost soothing in a way. No need to be alarmed. She was letting her imagination anticipate the worst. She would call him tomorrow. Meanwhile, a little space was a good thing, especially since she still regretted her impulse the night before. The intimacy of that call troubled her. She could acknowledge and deal with the glimmer of attraction she'd felt upon his return. But letting down her guard and inviting him into her innermost thoughts was a complication she didn't need at the moment.

Despite her resolve, his message continued to niggle as she put on the kettle and waited for the water to boil. The results of the DNA testing on the bracelet wouldn't be back for weeks so that couldn't be the reason for his call. She let her mind skip ahead to the possible outcome of those tests. If the blood embedded in the yarn belonged to Riley, then someone, possibly an accomplice, had held onto her bracelet all this time. If the blood belonged to Silas Creed, then maybe the Cavanaughs could finally have some sort of closure. Assuming, of course, the DNA could be matched. Silas Creed had at least one relative in the area. Surely he could be persuaded to provide a sample.

On and on her mind churned while she fixed the tea, made sure the house was locked up and then carried her cup upstairs to get ready for bed. Nestled under the covers, she sipped the chamomile and watched a mindless TV program on her tablet until she grew drowsy. Sam didn't call again. That was a good thing, she decided.

Finishing her drink, she unplugged and got up to brush her teeth. She stood at the window for a few minutes, watching the glint of moonlight on water. A breeze animated the shadows along the bank, causing her heart to thud with each movement. She stared hard into the night, but if anyone watched from afar, she didn't notice.

Climbing back into bed, she turned off the lamp and pulled up the covers. Despite the chamomile, she felt tense and out of sorts. Why couldn't things just go back to the way they'd been before the Unknown Caller had reached out to her? Before someone in a black parson's hat had appeared at the top of the embankment. Before the bracelet, before the peacock feather, before Sam Reece had come back into her life.

The monsters had been there all along, nipping at her heels, but somehow she'd managed to keep them at bay. Now they'd come slithering through her defenses, coiling and hissing at the fringes of her memory until she once again began to doubt herself. What had she seen that night?

She lay on her back and watched the shifting patterns on the ceiling until she finally dozed off. Her cell phone awakened her sometime later. She bolted upright in bed, still groggy and unsure of what she'd heard until the ringtone pealed again. She picked up the phone and peered at the screen. *Unknown Caller.*

Don't answer. Let it go to voice mail.

But she couldn't ignore the call any more than she could pretend everything had gone back to normal while she slept. She hit the accept button and lifted the phone to her ear.

"Hello?"

"Ellie?"

Riley? She almost said the name aloud before she caught herself. "Who is this?"

"Don't you recognize my voice?"

Ellie came wide-awake with another start. "Jenna?"

The ensuing silence went on for so long that Ellie thought the call might have dropped.

"Jenna? Are you there? Hello?"

"I'm here—"

Her voice cut out. Ellie pushed herself up against the headboard as she gripped the phone to her ear. "Hello? Hello?"

The voice sputtered to life. "Can you talk?"

By this time Ellie was thoroughly distressed. Jenna sounded strangely muffled, as if she were speaking from underneath the covers or inside a closet. As if she didn't want someone nearby to overhear. Strange that such a thought would even occur to her. A weak signal was the logical explanation.

She cleared her throat as she tried to clear her head. "Yes, of course I can talk. But you're breaking up a bit."

"Hold on." Another long pause. Then, "Is this better?"

"Yes, I can hear you now. But you're calling awfully late. Is everything okay?"

"It's late?" Jenna sounded confused. "I'm sorry. I sometimes lose track of time when I get like this."

Apprehension tingled along Ellie's spine. "Like what? What's wrong, Jen?"

Ellie heard a shuffling noise as if Jenna were moving around while they talked. Then she heard what sounded like another voice in the background.

"Jenna? Are you alone? Is someone there with you?"

"It's…no one."

Ellie was starting to get a very bad feeling about this phone call. She tried to remember the last time she'd spoken to Jenna. Must have been months ago. Had she been like this then? It wasn't unusual for her to sound vague and distracted, but this seemed different somehow, though Ellie couldn't put her finger on exactly what it was that bothered her. Maybe the late hour was cause enough to worry.

"Ellie?"

"I'm here, Jenna."

"I'm sorry I woke you up. You're not mad at me, are you?"

The uncertainty in her voice made her seem young and vulnerable. Ellie swallowed past a sudden lump in her throat as memories stirred. "I'm not at all mad. I just want to make sure you're okay."

"Can I ask you a question?"

"Of course. Anything."

Her voice dropped to a near whisper. "Do you ever think about that night?"

Ellie closed her eyes. "Yes. Every day of my life."

"Do you ever wonder…?" Jenna's words trailed away.

"What, Jen?"

"Why you weren't taken?"

The question was so softly spoken Ellie might have thought she'd dreamed it. She drew a breath and released it. "Every day of my life."

"Why me and not you?" There was a harder edge in Jenna's voice now.

Ellie gripped the phone. "I don't know. I've asked myself that same question a million times over. Maybe because my dad was the sheriff or because my brother came looking for me. We'll likely never know."

"Don't you think it strange that you and Tom were both spared? That you were the *only* ones spared?"

She asked the same question that any number of people in Belle Pointe had asked behind closed doors for the past fifteen years. Why had only Sheriff Brannon's kids been saved?

Ellie gave her friend the same answer that Tom had always given to her. "I don't think we were spared. I think we were both left for dead. Tom was hit in the back of the head so hard it took nearly thirty stitches to sew him up. When he came to, he found me lying facedown in the water. It's a miracle I didn't drown."

"But you didn't drown, did you? You lived."

"So did you, Jen."

"Did I? Sometimes I wonder. Maybe I'm not really here at all. Maybe I'm just a ghost lost in all this mist." Her voice was still soft and wistful but that underlying darkness worried Ellie.

"You're not a ghost. You're a survivor and you're stronger than you know," she said fiercely.

"I don't feel very strong tonight."

"What's wrong?" Ellie drew up her legs and huddled beneath the covers. "Has something happened?" When Jenna didn't answer, she started to panic. "Where are you calling from?"

"Why does that matter?" Jenna asked.

"I just want to make sure you're somewhere safe."

"I'm safe…for now."

"What does that mean, for now?"

"Nothing. It just means the future is always uncertain. Who would know that better than me? Can I ask you something else?"

Ellie braced herself. "What is it?"

"What do you remember about that night?"

She thought about how to respond. "We've talked about this before. I'm not sure it's a good idea to go over it now. It's very late."

"Please, Ellie. I've been having so many dreams lately. Just tell me what you remember once we got to the Ruins."

Ellie didn't want to talk about that night. She'd long ago come to the conclusion that it did no one any good to dwell on the past. But she could hardly deny Jenna's tremulous request. Maybe going over the details would somehow be cathartic this time. "We split up once we were inside. I went upstairs while you stayed below with Riley. I walked down the hallway, glancing in rooms until I heard a scream. I couldn't have been gone that long. It seemed like only minutes. I ran back downstairs to make sure you and Riley were okay. That's when I was grabbed from behind. I don't remember anything else until I woke up in the hospital."

"Are you sure you didn't see anyone there that night? Even just a glimpse?"

"Not that I can recall." Ellie paused. "Did you see someone?"

"Maybe. I'm not sure. I have all these images in my head, but I can't make sense of them. Everything seems so blurry and distant. Like I'm trying to peer through clouds."

"Yes. That's exactly the way it seems to me, too," Ellie said. "Tell me about these dreams you're having."

"I'm inside the Ruins. The moon looks blood red through the broken windows. I stand there, listening to the creaks and moans in that old place and I think about all the patients that once lived there. All the misery that must still be trapped there."

Ellie shivered. "Go on."

"I can hear the wind in the trees outside and the scream of a peacock down by the water. Cobwebs stick to my hair as I move across the room. *Shush.* Riley said she heard something." Her voice changed as she shifted verb tenses. Ellie wondered if she even noticed. "We thought she'd imagined the sound at first. She was so nervous about being there. You told her not to be a baby and then you left us and went upstairs."

She was no longer recounting a dream, but a memory. When she paused, Ellie could hear whispering somewhere nearby. She tensed.

"Jenna? Who's with you?"

"I told you. No one."

"I can hear someone whispering to you."

Another pause. "How do you know she's not whispering to you?"

Goose bumps popped along Ellie's arms. "She?"

"I don't hear anything," Jenna insisted. "It must be your imagination."

Was that a taunt? Ellie wondered.

"Where was I?" Jenna asked. "Oh, yes. Riley heard something. She was right, of course. Someone *was* there. After you went upstairs, she and I heard footsteps in one of the other rooms. Then we heard a door open and close. Riley said she saw someone staring at us from down the hallway. I figured it was just one of the older kids trying to scare us so I went to check it out. I told Riley to wait for me."

She and Riley had separated? This was new information to Ellie. "What else do you remember?"

"I don't remember anything. I'm telling you about my dream."

"What else do you remember about your dream?"

Another silence stretched before she said softly, "The floor is cold."

"The floor in the Ruins?"

Jenna ignored the question. "The floor is cold, but Riley's skin is burning up, like she's on fire from the inside."

Ellie's heart skipped a beat. Jenna was no longer inside the Ruins. She'd fast-forwarded to her and Riley's captivity. Ellie had never heard her talk about it before. As far as she knew, Jenna's memory of that time was a complete blank. Something must have been unleashed in her dreams. The images she'd conjured were so disturbing Ellie wasn't sure how to proceed. She didn't want to push, but neither did she want Jenna to retreat.

"Where are you in your dream?" she asked softly.

"I don't know. It's pitch black in here. I feel my way around the room over and over, but I can't find a door or window. Just bars. I think we're in a cell or a cage. No bed, no chairs. There's a bucket in the corner. You know. For when we need to go. After a few days, the smell gets really bad."

Ellie took several breaths. "What about food and water?"

"A little now and then. Not enough for Riley to get better. I've tried giving her my share, but she won't take it. She just gets weaker and weaker. She hasn't eaten anything in days and she no longer talks to me."

"Is she…?"

Jenna's voice hardened. "I don't want to talk about that."

"You don't have to talk about anything you don't want to," Ellie soothed.

"Don't hang up, okay?"

"I won't. I'm here for as long as you want me."

"Ellie?" The voice grew soft again.

"Yes?"

"I'm scared."

"In your dream?"

"No, in real life. I don't want to fall asleep. If I close my eyes, he'll come for me."

"Who, Jen?"

"Preacher." The word was spoken in a reverent whisper.

A wave of panic washed up through Ellie's chest and clogged her throat. For a moment, she allowed herself to be drawn into Jenna's delusion. What if Silas Creed really was alive? What if he'd been watching her, too? How else would he have known she would be at the Thayer house feeding the peacocks that morning?

With an effort, she reined in her paranoid thoughts. She needed to stay calm for Jenna's sake. "That's not possible. Silas Creed is dead. He can't hurt you anymore. He can't hurt anyone."

Jenna's voice rose. "You don't know that! No one can know that for sure. Except maybe Riley."

"Riley isn't coming back, either, Jen."

"Then why is she calling me? Why is she leaving clues on my front porch?"

"You mean the peacock feather?" Ellie swung her legs over the side of the bed and got up to pad over to the window. The moon was so bright she could see all the way across the lake. She trailed her gaze along the bank, searching through the shadows.

Jenna said sharply, "How did you know about the feather?"

"Agent Reece told me."

"When did you talk to Sam?"

Sam? "He came down to see me after you told him about the call that came into my live broadcast."

"Then he believed me?"

"About the call? Of course he did. I played him the recording."

"I don't mean that. Did he believe me about everything else? He must have. Why else would he have made the trip to Belle Pointe if he didn't think Riley was still alive?"

"I wouldn't read too much into that," Ellie cautioned. "It's his job to follow every lead, no matter how remote. I know you want to believe Riley is still alive. I do, too. But we have to be realistic. It's been fifteen years."

"I am being realistic," Jenna said stubbornly. "She's alive and she left that feather on my porch to prove it.

Somehow she's managed to get away and she's trying to warn us about Preacher."

"Jenna—" Ellie broke off abruptly as she moved closer to the window. She could see the dock of the empty fishing cabin across the moonlit lake. Two women sat on the edge, dangling their feet in the water. At least, Ellie had the impression they were female. She could make out the soft curves of their silhouettes and the outline of long hair down their backs. They sat very close, heads together, shoulders touching. As she watched, one of them got to her feet, quickly undressed and dove into the water. Ellie was so riveted by the scene that for a moment she could have sworn she heard the splash.

She pressed the phone against her ear. *Had* she heard the splash?

Jenna's voice broke into her reverie. "We have to find her, Ellie. Sam will do what he can, but you and I both know we're the only ones who can save her."

The woman in the water swam back to the dock and hitched herself up beside the other figure. Ellie watched from afar as her nerve endings bristled.

"Maybe we should meet and talk this through. Where are you, Jenna?"

Her voice grew petulant. "Why do you keep asking me that?"

"I told you. I want to make sure you're safe."

"And I told you, I'm safe for now. When do you want to meet?"

"Tomorrow is my day off. I can drive to Dallas first thing."

"No, don't do that."

"Why?"

The swimmer scooted closer so that their heads were together once again.

Ellie cradled her phone against her shoulder as she opened the window. Voices carried at night and over water. She leaned out, letting the night air stir her tangled hair. She listened closely, but the only sound that came to her was the breeze whispering through the leaves.

"Why don't you want me to drive to Dallas?" she asked.

"I'll come there," Jenna said. "Let's meet in town. I've been meaning to get back to Belle Pointe anyway. I'll text you later and we can figure out a time and place."

"Jenna?"

"Yes?"

"Are you sure you're alone?"

"I'm alone and never alone all at the same time. But I don't expect you to understand that."

"Jen—"

"Good night, Ellie."

She remained at the window as both figures rose. One of them started up the steps that led to the cabin. The other grabbed her clothes from the dock and glanced over her shoulder as she dressed. Ellie was too far away to know for certain, but she could have sworn the woman's gaze lifted to her bedroom window.

Chapter Nine

Ellie couldn't fall back asleep after her conversation with Jenna. So many disturbing things had come to light during the course of that call, not the least of which was the possibility that Jenna may have been sitting across the lake the whole time they'd spoken. But why?

Everyone in town knew the fishing cabin had been empty since the owner's death earlier in the summer. Anyone could have driven out to use the dock for a midnight swim. It made little sense that Jenna and her companion had come all the way from Dallas to go out to the cabin in the middle of the night.

But Ellie couldn't shake the suspicion that Jenna had been hiding something. Nor could she forget Jenna's *dream* revelations that seemed to have merged with her forgotten memories. Those dark images kept Ellie tossing and turning until dawn broke and she finally threw back the covers and got up. She worked around the house and in her office until midmorning when she received a text from Jenna. They agreed on a time and place to meet and then Ellie went back upstairs to shower and dress.

A little while later, she drove into town and found a parking place down the block from the restaurant. Located across the street from the Belle Pointe Inn, the Lantern Grill had been a staple in town for as long as Ellie could remember. The elegant eatery enjoyed a brisk dinner business, especially on weekends, but most people sought out the less expensive and more family-friendly atmosphere of the Corner Diner for lunch. Ellie had suggested the Lantern Grill for that very reason. She and Jenna could sit at a quiet table without being disturbed.

Jenna was already seated at the back of the restaurant by the time Ellie walked in. She looked lovely in a soft blue top that matched her eyes and complemented her blond hair. A stranger seeing her in passing would never have suspected the trauma she'd been through in her lifetime, but Ellie immediately noted the faint shadows beneath the blue eyes and the hollows in her pale cheeks. She'd lost weight since they'd last met.

Another young woman was seated beside her at the table. She was also blond, but with strawberry highlights and eyes more green than blue. Despite the summer heat, she was chicly dressed in black with large gold hoops in her earlobes. As Ellie approached the table, the woman leaned over to whisper something in Jenna's ear, reminding Ellie of the two silhouettes she'd spotted across the lake the night before.

She paused briefly beside the table to smile down at Jenna. They made no move to embrace. A tacit agreement had kept a formal distance between them for years.

"Hello, Jenna."

"Ellie! There you are!"

"I hope you haven't been waiting long." She slid into the chair directly across from Jenna. "You look lovely as always. What a beautiful top."

Jenna smoothed a hand across the silky fabric. "Hazel picked it out."

Ellie's gaze moved to the stranger.

"I'm sorry," Jenna said quickly. "You two haven't met yet, have you? Jenna, this is my roommate, Hazel Lamont. Hazel, this is—"

"You don't have to tell me who she is. I would know Ellie Brannon anywhere." She gave Ellie a long appraisal as she thrust her hand across the table. "You look just as I imagined."

Ellie wasn't quite sure what to make of the woman's gregarious greeting. Or the hint of slyness glinting in the green-blue eyes.

They shook hands. "This is quite a surprise. Jenna didn't mention that you would be driving down with her," Ellie said.

"I hope you don't mind my crashing your little party. I've been dying to meet you in person for a long, long time. Of course, I feel like I already know you. Jenna has told me *so* much about you."

Ellie wondered if the emphasis was meant to provoke a reaction. They'd only just met so any assessment on her part would be tainted by her suspicion that Hazel had been with Jenna on the dock of the fishing cabin last night. In the light of day, Ellie was less certain of what she'd seen—or whom she'd seen—but she couldn't shake the feeling that Hazel Lamont was more than she seemed.

A coy smile tugged at the corners of her lips as if she'd correctly interpreted Ellie's misgivings.

Ellie slung the strap of her bag over the back of the chair and did her best to relax. "When did you drive down? You must have gotten an early start."

"Oh, yes. We're both morning people, which makes for a harmonious living arrangement," Hazel said. "Wouldn't you agree, Jenna?"

Jenna nodded as she locked gazes with Ellie. "I would. There aren't many people I could live with these days, especially since I've come to realize how rare true friendship really is."

"Well said," Hazel murmured, her gaze also on Ellie.

Why do I feel ambushed? Ellie wondered. The vibe at the table was odd to say the least. But then the conversation with Jenna the night before hadn't exactly been normal.

"Hazel isn't just my roommate, she's my hero," Jenna added. "She's saved my life on more than one occasion."

"And you mine." They exchanged a glance and a smile. The intimacy between them didn't seem at all romantic, but certainly more than a casual friendship. They seemed to want Ellie to be aware of their closeness.

She took it all in from across the table, trying to keep her demeanor pleasant and her tone mildly curious. "How long have you known each other?"

Jenna unfolded her napkin. "Not as long as you and I, but long enough. We lost contact for several years. A mutual friend who knew that I was looking for a roommate put us back in touch."

"It was fate," Hazel declared as she propped her elbows on the table and rested her chin on folded hands. "But enough about us. Let's talk about you, Ellie. I've listened to your radio show with Jenna. You have some strange people calling in, but what a fascinating way to make a living."

"It has its moments. Other than my job, though, I'm a pretty boring subject."

"Just a simple, small-town girl," Hazel said, still with that hint of guile.

"Yes, pretty much. What do you do, Hazel?"

"Oh, look how you managed to turn the conversation back on me so quickly."

"You'll have to forgive my curiosity," Ellie said. "It isn't every day I get to meet Jenna's roommate."

"Then ask me whatever you like. I'm an open book. Mostly." She winked. "As for what I do, I'm between jobs at the moment. Luckily, I don't have to worry about finances."

"That is lucky," Ellie said. "Where did you two meet?"

Hazel turned to Jenna. "Should I tell her the story or should we keep her guessing?"

"Now I think you have to tell me," Ellie said.

Hazel seemed to consider. "Maybe later."

The server appeared with glasses of water and menus. Hazel said briskly, "We'll need some time. We're still catching up."

"Let me know when you're ready." The young woman discreetly faded away.

Hazel fiddled with one of her earrings, drawing Ellie's attention to the large moonstone on her right hand. Recognition stirred and for a moment the milky iridescence seemed to mesmerize her. Riley had once had a ring very similar to the one on Hazel Lamont's finger. She'd stopped wearing it one day and claimed she'd lost it. When Ellie had offered to help her search, she'd mumbled something about the ring bringing her bad luck anyway. For someone so young, Riley had been awfully superstitious.

"She recognizes it."

Hazel's voice drew Ellie back with a start. "What?"

A smug smile flashed before Hazel glanced at Jenna. "See? I told you she'd remember."

Ellie felt an irrational urge to snatch the ring off the woman's finger. She tamped down the compulsion as she studied Jenna's expression. "That can't be Riley's ring. She told me she lost it."

Jenna's smile was a fleeting imitation of Hazel's. "She didn't lose it. She gave it to me."

Ellie frowned. "Then why would she tell me she lost it?"

Jenna's eyes glittered with something dark and unpleasant. "She didn't want you to know. You always loved her things so much. Her clothes, her shoes. Especially her jewelry. She was afraid if she told you she'd given the ring to me, you'd be angry."

"Why would I be angry?"

"Come on, Ellie. You were always jealous of my relationship with Riley."

Ellie felt blindsided by the accusation. "That's not true. I loved you both like sisters. I'm stunned that you would think otherwise."

Jenna merely shrugged. "I guess we remember things differently."

"I guess we do."

"It *is* a beautiful ring." Hazel waggled her fingers. The moonstone shimmered mockingly at Ellie. "I don't blame you for coveting it."

"I never—" Ellie broke off, turning her attention back to Jenna. "Maybe this wasn't such a good idea after all. I think another day might be better for our discussion."

"Oh, I'm sorry. Am I in the way?" Hazel asked innocently, but Ellie had the feeling she wasn't sorry at all. The uncomfortable vibe she'd detected earlier had turned into an antagonistic undercurrent.

"I just think it might be better for Jenna and me to discuss certain things in private."

Jenna bristled. "We can talk in front of Hazel. I trust her with my life."

All well and good, Ellie thought. But she wasn't sure she trusted Hazel Lamont with hers.

She was wondering how to gracefully exit the table when she spotted Sam Reece at the front of the restaurant. Their gazes connected and he nodded briefly before he started toward their table. Ellie didn't say anything until he was almost upon them and then she looked up in relief, happier to see him than the situation warranted. She noted his suit and tie, and decided he must still be on the FBI clock even though it was Saturday.

Across the table, Jenna visibly started when she saw him. Her hand flew to her heart as her gaze lifted. "Agent Reece! What a surprise to see you here."

"I'm a little taken aback myself." He glanced around the table, his gaze lingering on Ellie before he shifted his focus back to Jenna. "I was across the street at the inn when I saw Ellie come inside. I decided to try to catch up with her."

"Is everything okay?" Ellie asked anxiously.

"Yes. Just a matter or two I wanted to talk over with you." He searched her face, his eyes smoldering with mystery. She couldn't deny the impact he had on her and wondered if anyone else had noticed. She took a quick survey. Jenna stared back at her, frowning.

"You two are on a first-name basis?" she demanded.

"No," Ellie said a little too quickly. "That is, I'm not." Why did she feel so defensive, all of a sudden? So intensely aware of Sam Reece staring down at her?

Hazel loudly cleared her throat. "I don't think we've met. At least not in person."

Before Jenna could make the introductions, Sam said, "You must be Hazel."

She extended her hand, gazing up at him through long, thick lashes. "And you're the famous Agent Reece. Jenna has spoken of you often. How wonderful to finally put a face with that deep voice." She leaned over and whispered something in Jenna's ear, causing her roommate to nod as her frown deepened.

Ellie couldn't help noticing that Sam kept his contact with Hazel brief. He dropped his hand to his side as he said to Jenna, "You didn't mention you were planning a trip to Belle Pointe the last time we spoke."

"It was sudden. Ellie suggested we meet." She made it sound like an accusation.

Ellie tried to shrug off her qualms as she addressed Jenna's claim. "After you called last night, I thought it a good idea that we talk in person."

"And here we all are," Hazel said cheerfully.

Sam's gaze was on Ellie again. She glanced away, more rattled by his attention than she wanted to admit.

"Won't you join us, Agent Reece?" Hazel invited. "Or do you prefer Sam?"

"Agent Reece is fine."

Hazel's tone shifted imperceptibly. "In any case, you'd be a welcome distraction. The conversation had taken an awkward turn when you came up. Sit down and I'll tell you all about it."

He lifted a brow at Ellie. She scooted over to the next chair, allowing him to sit across from Jenna. Ellie was now seated across from Hazel. The roommate gave her a knowing look, which Ellie had no idea how to interpret.

"Jenna and Hazel were just about to tell me how and where they met," Ellie said, before Hazel could mention the ring.

"Why is that awkward?" he asked.

"I guess it all depends on your perspective," Hazel replied. "We met at the Penn Shepherd Hospital in Dallas. I believe you're familiar with the facility, Agent Reece?"

"I am, yes."

"The Penn Shepherd Hospital," Ellie murmured. "Isn't that where—"

"They lock away the crazy people? Again, depends on your perspective." Hazel was still smiling but her gaze on Ellie had darkened. "I was a patient there when Jenna was admitted."

Jenna put her hand on Hazel's arm, but she gently brushed it away. "It's all right, Jenny. We're among friends." Her gaze slid back to Sam. "Maybe Agent Reece would be interested in knowing why I was there."

"Only if you feel like talking about it," he said.

"Yes, I think I do." Her eyes glittered dangerously. "When I was sixteen, my parents were brutally murdered by an intruder as they lay sleeping in their bed one night. For a while, the FBI agent assigned to the case considered me a suspect."

"Why was the FBI involved in a homicide investigation?" Sam asked.

"I'm sure it had something to do with my father's business affiliations, if you get my drift."

"When and where did this happen?"

Ellie marveled at Sam's calm response. She felt stunned by the revelation and was almost certain her eyes, if not her entire body, reflected the shock.

"Sixteen years ago at our home in Westlake."

"Ritzy neighborhood," Sam noted.

"You can look it up. Ken and Cynthia Lamont. Anyway, my uncle, who had been appointed my guardian, decided that I was having trouble coping with the loss. Acting out, as he called it. He thought a nice long stay in a psychiatric hospital might help me deal with my emotions. My incarceration also gave him ample time and opportunity to steal a sizable portion of my inheritance."

Sam remained unfazed. "That's quite a story."

"I thought you might enjoy it."

Ellie wondered if even a word of it was true.

"As luck would have it, when Jenny came to the hospital, the only available bed was in my room." Hazel's gaze moved back to Ellie. She looked quite pleased with herself. "We became fast friends. *Sisters.* We told each other *everything.*"

"How long were you roommates?" Sam asked.

She sat back in her chair, somehow managing to look bored and amused at the same time. "A few months. At some point, the staff decided we needed to be separated. They claimed I was a bad influence, if you can imagine such a thing."

I can, Ellie thought. With very little effort.

"But you weren't," Jenna said fervently. "You were my only friend in that awful place. I couldn't stand being there after they moved me."

"We're together now," Hazel soothed. "That's all that matters. And no one will ever separate us again. *No one.*"

Ellie and Sam exchanged a worried glance, which seemed to agitate Jenna. She sat forward suddenly. "I'd like to know what you're doing to find Riley, Agent Reece. I have a right to know about your investigation."

He answered cautiously. "I've made some inquiries."

"What kind of inquiries?"

He sat back as he studied the table. "Has either of you been contacted by a woman named Melanie Kent?"

Ellie started. "You found her?"

"Who's Melanie Kent?" Hazel leaned in, mimicking Jenna's posture. It was disconcerting to see the two of them together. Hazel seemed overbearing and protective, her larger-than-life persona completely overshadowing the reserved Jenna. Yet Ellie had the strangest notion that the real power in the friendship belonged to Jenna.

"Melanie Kent published a book about the kidnapping several years ago," Sam explained. "Apparently she's writing a sequel." He got out his phone and scrolled through the camera roll. Then he turned his phone so that Jenna could see the screen. "Do you recognize this photograph?"

Jenna stared at the image for the longest time. "When did you take that?"

"I didn't. I found it tacked to the wall of a converted garden shed where Melanie Kent has been staying." He rotated the phone toward Ellie. "She has several candid shots of you on that wall, as well."

Ellie frowned. "She's been taking pictures of us without our knowing? Why?"

Sam shrugged. "I'm sure she'd call it research. My guess is she's been at it for weeks."

Hazel reached over and snatched the phone, using her fingertips to enlarge the image. "I remember that day. You'd just moved in, Jenny. Your parents had come to help unload all the boxes. You walked them outside and sat down on the porch to watch them leave."

"When was this?" Sam asked.

"A couple of weeks ago at least. Sometimes it's hard to keep track. Days tend to run together even out in the real world."

"You said she's staying in a converted garden shed?" Ellie asked. "That seems a little strange."

"Not as strange as you might think." Sam placed his phone on the table. "Which brings me to my next question. How well do you remember Cory Small?"

"He was a student at Belle Pointe High School at the time of the kidnapping," Ellie said. "He would have been going into his senior year at the end of that summer."

"What else?" Sam asked.

"He's Silas Creed's nephew. I barely knew who he was before the kidnapping, but afterward, he and his mother were all anyone in town could talk about. I came to feel very sorry for them. All those ugly accusations and gossip must have taken a toll. He transferred to another school before the start of his senior year. I didn't keep up with him after that."

"He runs the family farm and a landscape nursery south of Belle Pointe," Sam said. "I drove out there yesterday to have a chat with him."

Jenna's eyes widened. "Why did you want to talk to him? Do you think he knows something about Riley?"

"Not necessarily. There's always been the question of whether or not someone helped Silas Creed leave town. Small still denies that either he or his mother was involved."

"Of course he would deny it," Hazel muttered.

Ellie's father had thoroughly investigated the Smalls after Silas Creed disappeared. He'd found no evidence that either had been in any way complicit, but there were those in town who had already passed judgment. People needed someone to blame and Silas Creed's family became an easy target. Ellie could only imagine the bad memories stirred by Sam's visit.

"I've no reason to believe he's done anything wrong," Sam said. "But I'm curious if either of you remember anything out of the ordinary."

Jenna shrugged. "I'm sorry. Nothing comes back to me."

"Are you sure? Think hard." Hazel placed her hand over Jenna's. "Didn't you once tell me there was an older boy in high school who had a thing for Riley?"

Jenna grew nervous and snatched her hand away. "How could I tell you about something I don't even remember?"

Hazel's voice dropped to a soothing monotone. "No worries. I must be mistaken. The name sounds a little familiar to me, too, but maybe I heard it from someone else."

Sam's gaze narrowed in puzzlement. "Who besides Jenna would have talked to you about Cory Small? Or about Riley, for that matter?"

"Maybe it was the reporter you mentioned earlier," Hazel suggested. "Melanie something-or-other."

"I didn't say she's a reporter."

Her gaze faltered. "Well, whatever she is, maybe she mentioned this Cory Small person."

"Then you have talked to her?" Sam pressed.

"It's possible," Hazel said with an ambiguous shrug. "She's obviously been hanging around our house."

"But you don't remember speaking with her?"

Hazel sighed. "I'm bored now. I don't want to talk about this anymore."

Sam's phone beeped. He glanced at Ellie, silently communicating the weirdness of the conversation before he picked up his cell. He read the text message, then pocketed his phone. "Would you excuse me? I need to make a quick call."

Ellie nodded. "Of course."

"Hurry back," Hazel drawled.

Jenna seemed hardly to notice his absence. Her gaze was on Ellie. She still looked upset, but there was something hard glittering beneath the faraway gaze.

Ellie wanted to find out more about an older boy's crush on Riley, but she hesitated to distress Jenna. She seemed to hover on a dangerous precipice, anxious and reticent one moment, hardened and resentful the next. Maybe it would be better to let Sam handle the questioning.

She pushed back her chair. "This seems like a good time to visit the ladies' room. Would you excuse me, too?"

Hazel gave a lethargic wave. "Take your time."

Ellie glanced back as she moved away from the table. The two heads were together again as Hazel spoke animatedly in Jenna's ear. Then she slowly turned and winked, as if she'd known all along that Ellie would be watching. As if the two of them shared some deep, dark secret. A chill shot through Ellie as she whirled and started toward the front of the restaurant.

She glimpsed Sam through the large plate glass window. His expression was intense as he stood in the shade, phone to his ear. Ellie wondered about the text message that had prompted what appeared to be an urgent call. She wondered a lot of things about Sam Reece. Why hadn't he told her earlier about his conversation with Cory Small?

Which brought her back to Hazel's disturbing claim. If Jenna had been aware of an older boy's interest in Riley, why hadn't Ellie known about it? The three friends had always confided in each other about boys, parents and everything else. Cory Small had been a rising senior that summer. Getting hit on by an older guy wasn't something a fifteen-year-old girl would have kept from one of her best friends. Or so Ellie wanted to believe.

But it seemed Riley and Jenna had kept other things from her, as well. She'd certainly been clueless about the moonstone ring. Had she really been the type of person in whom neither of her closest friends thought they could confide?

Inside the ladies' room, she stood at the sink, going through the motions of washing her hands, tightening her ponytail and reapplying her lipstick. She didn't want to go back out to the table. Jenna's erratic behavior was more than a little troubling. *And don't get me started on Hazel.*

After applying a second coat of lipstick, she took her time putting everything back in her bag. The door opened as she stood contemplating her reflection. Hazel sauntered in, looking as sleek as a cat in expensive black jeans and a fitted tank top. Ellie watched her suspiciously in the mirror. The enigmatic woman moved toward the stalls but didn't go inside one. Instead she stood behind Ellie so that their reflected gazes met. Ellie felt a tingle of apprehension but she tried not to show it. Tried not to worry that she was alone in the bathroom with a woman who may or may not have murdered her parents.

"Barely There," Hazel said.

Ellie stared at her in confusion. "I'm sorry?"

"The name of your lipstick. Barely There. Am I right?"

Ellie fished the lipstick from her bag and glanced at the bottom of the tube. "How did you know that?"

"Jenna has worn that same neutral shade for years, even though I tell her it's too bland for someone with her looks. She's attractive enough to go for a much bolder color. The shade suits you, though."

The dig might have amused Ellie if she hadn't found the woman's performance so unnerving. And it was a performance, Ellie was almost certain.

Hazel cocked her head, still watching her in the mirror. "You don't wear much makeup, do you? Don't fuss with your hair or bother with your clothes." Her gaze took in Ellie's simple sleeveless dress and sandals. "Just a simple small-town girl."

"We've already established I'm a boring subject." Ellie looped her bag over her shoulder as she turned from the mirror. "Do you have a problem with me?" she asked bluntly.

Hazel shrugged. "Why would I have a problem with you? I know exactly who and what you are. You seem to have Agent Reece fooled, though."

"I'm sorry, what?"

Hazel tossed back her hair. "I saw the way he looked at you just now. Jenny saw it, too. You must know how she feels about him. Why would you flaunt your relationship in front of her?"

Ellie stared at her in stunned disbelief. "I have no idea what you're talking about. I don't have a relationship with Agent Reece. I hardly know him."

"So you say. But I happen to know the two of you have been spending a lot of time together lately."

The revelation made Ellie uneasy and borderline frightened, but she tried not to show it. "How would you know that? Have you been watching my house?"

Hazel's eyes flared. "So you admit Sam Reece has been out to your place recently."

"Didn't Jenna tell you? He came to see me because she was worried about the phone call that came into my radio broadcast."

"Of course she told me. She tells me everything." Hazel moved up to one of the mirrors, running fingers through her strawberry tresses. "If anyone were to ever hurt her again, I just don't know what I would do."

Ellie hated confrontations, especially an unfair attack from a woman she'd only just met. Her first instinct was to walk away, but instead she leaned back against the counter as she met Hazel's gaze straight on.

"Why on earth would you think I'd ever hurt Jenna? She's my friend, too."

"A true friend would never have left her that night."

The accusation stung no matter the accuser. "I didn't leave her."

"Oh, right. You were rendered unconscious. Tossed down a hill and left for dead. Or so you say. But, conveniently, your brother was the only one who could corroborate your story."

"It wasn't a story. It was the truth."

Hazel's voice rose menacingly. "You have no idea what she went through. You may think you do, but you don't." She turned on the faucet and vigorously scrubbed her hands, as if trying to wash away something tainted. "It was storming the night they brought her into my ward. I remember the flashes of lightning through the windows and how the thunder helped to drown out her screams."

Dear God, her screams?

Ellie suppressed a shudder as she studied Hazel's reflection. The enigmatic woman wasn't so much beautiful as striking, the reddish-blond mane framing a long, narrow face dominated by those aqua eyes. Like Jenna, she was thin almost to the point of gauntness, but her arms looked toned, her hips and thighs sinewy beneath the fitted jeans. The image of a jungle cat once again came to mind. Fast, sleek and deadly.

Their gazes met once more and Hazel's smile sent a fresh chill rippling along Ellie's nerve endings.

"Jenny was like a wild thing that night, like something had come completely unleashed inside her. The orderlies had to hold her down to sedate her. Then they had to strap her to the bed because when the drugs wore off, she tried to pull out her hair and claw off her skin. They left her in my room even when another bed opened up because I was the only one who could calm her. I sat with her night and day. I held her hand for hours. I was there for her when no one else wanted to come near her, including her own parents. Including *you.*"

Ellie's blood ran cold with shock. Every word Hazel spoke was like a knife thrust into her heart. "I came to the hospital to see her. At first, they wouldn't let anyone in, and then later, she…didn't want visitors. Not for months. But I'm glad she had you. You were a good friend to her."

"We were so much more than friends. I don't expect someone like you to understand, but Jenny became a part of me. When they took her away, it was like they'd cut out a piece of me."

"Why did they take her away?" Ellie couldn't help asking.

"I told you. They thought I was a bad influence. They put her in another wing and wouldn't let me see her because one of her doctors decided I was feeding her delusions. I wasn't feeding her anything." She dried her hands just as forcefully. "She wanted desperately to believe that Riley was still alive and so I gave her hope. I still do."

Ellie frowned. "By convincing her Riley is still alive? What happens when she finds out otherwise?"

"She won't because Riley isn't dead."

"How can you possibly know that?"

Hazel paused, cocking her head as she searched her reflection. "You really don't understand, do you?"

For a moment, Ellie wasn't sure if Hazel had addressed her or an invisible third party that only she could see. "Understand what?"

Hazel peered more closely into the mirror, turning her head first one way and then the other. She seemed fascinated by her own image. "Do you know Jenny's parents?"

Ellie checked the door, wishing someone else would walk through. The more time she spent alone in Hazel's company, the more unsettled she became. Yet she couldn't seem to tear herself away from a conversation that both fascinated and repelled her. "I used to. They moved to Fort Worth after the kidnapping to be closer to Jenna's doctor."

"Is that what they told you? That's funny. Jenna said they moved away because of you."

Was that true? Ellie wondered. The Malloys had sold their beautiful home and left town because of her? Because they blamed her for what happened?

A wave of nausea washed over her, even though she told herself to take anything Hazel Lamont revealed with a grain of salt. Hazel was obviously the one who had a bone to pick with Ellie, not the Malloys.

"They've never accepted the fact that their daughter is all grown up. They still forbid her to associate with the *wrong* people." Hazel air-quoted in disgust. "It seems we have more in common than you think."

Ellie really hoped that wasn't true. Hazel Lamont

seemed unstable and vindictive, a treacherous combination.

She was still watching Ellie in the mirror. "Her parents took her away from Penn Shepherd without letting us say goodbye. Jenny was there one day and poof… gone the next." Her eyes took on the same faraway look Ellie had noted in Jenna's. "They wouldn't even let her write to me. No visits, no phone calls. There's always a way, though. I didn't forget Jenny and she never forgot me. When I was able, I used some of my inheritance to buy a house in a nice, quiet neighborhood. Then I went to rescue Jenny."

"Rescue her?"

Hazel turned with that disturbing smile. "Yes, rescue. Her parents now know there isn't anything they can do to keep us apart. You should probably know that, too." She moved in closer, forcing Ellie to take a reluctant step back. "I'll let you in on a little secret."

Ellie swallowed. "What's that?"

"You may know how to deal with the freaks and weirdos that call into your radio show, but you've never dealt with anyone like me."

Chapter Ten

Sam was alone at the table when Ellie came back. He rose as she approached. She looked around, perplexed. "Where's Jenna?"

"She got a text message and rushed out of here. She said to tell you she'd call you later." He paused. "Everything okay? You look upset."

"I just had a run-in with Hazel Lamont in the bathroom. I'm sure the text message Jenna received was from her."

Sam touched her elbow briefly. "What happened? What did she say to you?"

"I'll tell you outside." She threw some bills on the table, even though they hadn't yet ordered. "Let's get out of here. I've lost my appetite."

They wound their way through the maze of tables, pausing outside the door while Sam scanned the street.

"Are you expecting someone?" Ellie asked anxiously as she moved into the shade of the building. The late summer sun beat down on the concrete walkway and she was still feeling a little queasy from the confrontation with Hazel.

Sam lifted a hand to shade his eyes briefly before he stepped back beside her. "You didn't happen to see what kind of car Jenna and Hazel were in, did you?"

"No, they were already inside the restaurant when I got here. Why?"

He looked uneasy. "A beige sedan has been tailing me for the past two days. I'm trying to figure out who the vehicle belongs to."

Ellie stared at him in confusion. "You think the car belongs to either Jenna or Hazel?"

"It's just a hunch." His attention was still riveted on the street. "I haven't been able to get a good look at the driver or the plate number."

Ellie glanced over her shoulder. She couldn't seem to help herself. It was the middle of the day. People were out and about. No reason to feel afraid and yet she couldn't shake the chill that had deepened with every word Hazel Lamont had uttered.

"You must have a reason for your hunch," she said.

He answered reluctantly. "Nothing specific, but their behavior has been troubling lately."

"*Their* behavior? I thought today was the first time you'd met Hazel."

"In person, yes. She called two nights ago from Jenna's phone. I was downtown at the time. When I asked to speak to Jenna, she wouldn't put her on. She said Jenna wasn't feeling herself. Before the call ended, I could have sworn I saw Jenna's reflection in a building window. She stood across the street with a phone to her ear. By the time the traffic cleared, she'd disappeared."

Ellie flashed back to the silhouettes on the dock

across the lake. Had they been following her, too? "Are you sure it was Jenna?"

"Call it a strong suspicion."

"Was that night the first time you'd spoken to Hazel on the phone?"

"As far as I know."

Ellie frowned. "As far as you know?"

"This may also sound odd, but I wasn't sure Hazel Lamont was a real person until today. Jenna has called and pretended to be someone else before."

Ellie stared at him in shock. "Who does she pretend to be?"

"She's never given me a name. Sometimes she pretends she's called a wrong number."

"Doesn't her name and number show up on your caller ID?"

"I'm guessing she uses a burner."

"Then how do you know it's her?"

"Call it another strong suspicion."

Ellie leaned back against the wall. "Why would she go to all that trouble? Buy another phone, call you and pretend to be someone else?"

"Only Jenna can answer that question."

Had Jenna ever called her under an assumed name? Ellie wondered. Melanie Kent had easily duped her years ago by adopting a fake persona. Ellie liked to think she was more savvy and insightful after a decade on the airwaves, but could she really know the true identities of her callers? How could she really know what Jenna had been up to since her parents had removed her from the Penn Shepherd Psychiatric Hospital years ago?

"Can I ask you a personal question?"

Sam glanced at her warily. "What is it?"

"Do you think Jenna has romantic feelings for you?"

He tried to shrug off the possibility, but Ellie saw his mouth tighten imperceptibly. "She certainly has boundary issues and she can become too dependent too quickly, which is why I had to set rules regarding when and where she can contact me."

"Maybe that's why she sometimes pretends to be someone else. To get around those boundaries." Ellie paused. "I can see why the hospital wanted to keep her away from Hazel. That woman strikes me as someone who knows how to exploit a person's weaknesses. I don't trust her. She seems the very definition of a loose cannon."

"I have my concerns, as well," Sam said. "I'll make some calls and find out what I can about her background."

"Thank you." Ellie kept going over that conversation with Hazel Lamont. The more she thought about it, the more convinced she became that Jenna's roommate was dangerously unstable and obsessively possessive. Ellie shuddered to think what might happen if Jenna had once again fallen under Hazel's influence.

She tucked loose strands of hair behind her ears as she watched the traffic in front of the restaurant. "About that beige sedan. Can't you check to see if a vehicle matching that description is registered to Hazel or Jenna?"

"I can, but if the car is a rental, it'll take longer to track down without a license plate number."

Something occurred to Ellie as he responded. "Wait a minute," she said slowly. "If you saw the beige sedan in Belle Pointe yesterday, then Jenna could already have been in town when she called. Maybe I really did see her and Hazel on the dock last night, although I have no idea why they would have gone out to the fishing cabin at that hour."

Sam leaned a shoulder against the wall. "You've lost me. What dock? What fishing cabin?"

"Oh, right. You don't know about that yet. There's an empty fishing cabin across the lake from me. I think I saw Jenna and Hazel on the dock last night while she was on the phone with me. I'd like to drive out there and see if they left anything behind. If you feel like riding along, I'll tell you about my conversation with Hazel on the way."

He nodded. "Sure. But let's take my car instead. I'll drive, you talk."

"What about my car?"

"I'll bring you back later to pick it up."

Ellie hesitated, a little disconcerted by the notion of being alone in the close confines of a vehicle with Sam Reece. Then she chided herself for having such a ridiculous and immature reaction. "We'll need to take the bridge across the lake. I'll give you directions as we go."

"Just give me a minute to change my clothes and bring the car around. Unless you'd like to wait for me in the inn."

"No, that's okay." She nodded down the street toward the town square. "I'll find a bench in the shade and wait for you there."

"Are you sure? It's awfully hot out here."

"I won't melt."

She waited until he'd crossed the street and disappeared inside the inn and then hitching her bag over her shoulder, she strolled along the sidewalk until she came to the town square. The stores were crowded with weekend shoppers. She found a bench in the shade where she could sit and people watch.

Directly across the street was the shadowy entrance to Ghost Alley, so named for the stories that cropped up from time to time about phantom lights and eerie whispers. In middle school, she, Jenna and Riley used to meet in the tiny cemetery located between the buildings and read ghost stories aloud. How quaint and innocent it all seemed now, sitting in the grass beside the old graves, goose bumps prickling their napes. No inkling of the real horror coming their way.

Ellie had fallen so deeply into her reverie that the ping of a text message startled her. Thinking Sam was probably ready to go, she hauled out her phone and glanced at the screen. There was a number but no name. The message read, Do you want to know what really happened to Riley? Call me.

Ellie shivered in the heat as she glanced both ways down the street. She told herself the message was just more of the same. An anonymous prankster was messing with her. But she couldn't ignore the possibility, no matter how remote, that the person who had sent the text might really know something about Riley's disappearance.

She tapped the number and lifted the phone to her

ear. After two rings, a female voice answered. "Ellie Brannon?"

"Yes. Who is this?"

"You don't recognize my voice?"

Ellie frowned as she shifted the phone to her other ear. "Should I?"

"We've spoken before on numerous occasions. I'm surprised you don't remember me."

Jenna? Hazel? The voice did sound vaguely familiar, but how could she be sure of anyone anymore? "I don't like games. Why won't you just tell me your name?"

"All in good time. Are you alone?"

Apprehension niggled. "Why does that matter?"

"I don't want any cops or FBI agents hanging around when we meet in person."

Ellie clutched the phone. "What makes you think I'll agree to meet you?"

"Do you want to know what happened to Riley or don't you?"

She tried to keep her voice neutral as she searched the street. "How can you possibly know what happened to Riley?"

"I've been investigating Riley Cavanaugh's disappearance for the past fifteen years. I've made solving her case my life's work. You'd be surprised how much I know." The voice went silent for a moment, allowing Ellie time to digest the disturbing claim. "When I end this call, put your phone back in your bag and get up from the bench. Casually. Don't call attention to yourself."

Ellie squinted across the sunny street, wondering

if someone watched her from behind a store window. "Where are you? Who are you?"

The caller ignored her questions. "After you put the phone away, enter the alley and go all the way back to the cemetery. Wait for me inside the gate."

"You must think I'm crazy," Ellie said. "Why would I do that?"

"You live alone on Echo Lake. Twice a day, you walk to an abandoned house to feed a dead woman's peacocks. You leave your studio at midnight with nothing but woods and water surrounding you. If I wanted to hurt you, I could have done so long before now. I just want to talk."

"Then tell me your name."

"Marie," she said softly. "My name is Marie Nightingale."

A wave of anger and panic washed over Ellie as she glanced around the square, frantically searching for Melanie Kent. A few passersby caught her eye and nodded. She told herself to calm down. Nothing was going to happen to her in the middle of town in broad daylight. Melanie Kent might be a ruthless, ambitious reporter who thought nothing of manufacturing evidence or a new identity to get a story, but she wasn't lethal. She posed no physical harm.

"Hello?" Ellie said into the phone. "Are you still there? Hello?"

The call had ended. Ellie rose from the bench and took a moment to contemplate her next move before she crossed the street and entered the alley. She'd waited years for the opportunity to tell Melanie Kent what she thought of her. But more important than airing past grievances was the need to know what the woman was up to in the here and now. What had brought her back to Belle Pointe at precisely this moment in time and why was she skulking about, taking pictures of Ellie and Jenna?

And what did she really know about Riley?

Ellie paused inside the alley to send a brief text to Sam, letting him know where to meet her. Then glancing over her shoulder, she put away the phone and headed toward the cemetery.

It was cool and dim in the shade of the buildings. Ellie was anxious but not afraid. People often used the alley as a shortcut over to the next street. This time of day, she was likely to encounter any number of people. Nothing was going to happen. She would be on guard the whole time. If she didn't like what Melanie Kent had to say or if her behavior seemed suspect, Ellie would leave at once.

A latticework gate opened into the tiny cemetery. The dozen or so graves had been left from a larger burial ground that was excavated and moved to the edge of town when Belle Pointe began to expand at the turn of the last century.

Ellie hesitated with her hand on the latch and then, taking a breath, she opened the gate and stepped through. She didn't see anyone at first. The park-like setting was shady and cool and she could hear the tinkle of a water feature nearby. She moved inside and glanced around. A woman sat on one of the benches with her back to the entrance. When she heard the latch click, she rose and turned to face Ellie.

A decade had passed since Ellie had last seen Melanie Kent. The years hadn't been particularly kind to the woman. Or maybe it was just the situation. She looked nervous and flighty, her feverish gaze darting from Ellie to the gate and then back. She wiped her hands down the sides of her jeans as she regarded Ellie from across the graves. She wore a floppy white hat that shaded her face and an oversize shirt that hid the thin contours of her body. As Ellie took a step toward her, Melanie's hand slipped to the backpack that rested beside her on the bench.

"It's been a long time," she said and then cleared her throat awkwardly as if she were having trouble coming up with the proper response. "How have you been, Ellie?"

"Are we really going to do this?" Ellie demanded. "Try to make small talk as if meeting in a cemetery after all these years is perfectly normal behavior?"

"Brass tacks, then." Melanie looked relieved. She pulled off her hat and tossed it on the bench, then ran fingers through her flattened hair to fluff it. "I'm a little surprised you agreed to see me."

"I'm a little surprised myself," Ellie said as she moved into the cemetery. A stray breeze ruffled tendrils at her temples and she tucked back the strands impatiently. "Don't make the mistake of thinking all is forgiven. I haven't forgotten what you did or how you played me. All those lies you told. The fake tears." She shook herself before anger toppled her defenses. "But that's not why I'm here. At least, it's not the main reason I'm here. You said you know what happened to Riley."

"It still haunts you, doesn't it? The not knowing." The subtle taunt seemed more like the old Melanie.

"Of course it does. Unlike you, I have real emotions." Ellie struggled at that moment to curtail those said emotions.

"Including regret?"

Ellie closed her eyes and counted to five. "Just tell me what you know about Riley."

Melanie moved to the side of the bench and perched a hip against the armrest. Reaching behind her, she pulled the backpack closer, as if afraid a ghost might make off with the contents. "You have to promise that nothing of what you learn here will leave these gates."

Ellie frowned. "I can't make that promise. If you know something about Riley's disappearance, then the authorities will need to be notified."

"Even if telling them would put my life in danger?"

"From whom?"

Her gaze darted again to the gate. "I'm not ready to name names. I need to put some protections in place first. Do you know what a dead man's switch is?"

"Yes, of course. That's a little dramatic, don't you think? But then, drama has always been your specialty."

Something flickered in the woman's fierce eyes. She took another glance around the cemetery as if to make certain they were still alone. Ellie wanted to believe her wariness was just an act. Melanie Kent was every bit the performer that Hazel Lamont was. Yet the woman's cautious behavior was contagious. Ellie found herself fighting the urge to glance over her shoulder.

"As you well know, I've been working on Riley's case for most of my adult life. I've conducted hundreds of interviews and amassed digital mountains of research." Melanie held up her thumb and forefinger, leaving a miniscule gap. "I'm this close to putting it all together."

"Then you don't really know what happened to Riley, do you? You're only guessing."

"It's more than guesswork. I know what happened that night. I can't prove it beyond a shadow of a doubt. Not yet. But I *know.*" Her voice dropped. "I may even know where to find the remains."

Ellie gasped. "What?"

The reporter's gaze softened unexpectedly. "You didn't really think she'd still be alive after all this time, did you?"

"No, of course not." But the idea of fifteen-year-old Riley hidden and alone for so many years tore at Ellie's heart. She tried to dispel the heartbreaking images, warning herself again to be wary of Melanie's machinations. "Tell me what you actually know. No theories, no guesswork, just facts."

The reporter nodded. "All right, then. We'll start slow and work our way to the finish. If I blurt everything out at once, you may have trouble absorbing the truth. It's…disturbing to say the least."

Ellie rubbed her bare arms and nodded.

Melanie rose but made no move to breach the distance between them. "If you want to know more after today, we can schedule another meeting. Discreetly, of course. Right now, I'm prepared to give you only a small taste of what I've uncovered. Do you understand and agree to my conditions?"

"I understand you only too well," Ellie said. "Can we just get on with it?"

"Did you know that Riley and Jenna had a falling out before you went to the Ruins that night?"

Ellie didn't know whether to be relieved or angry. She'd mentally braced herself for a horrifying revelation. Instead Melanie was presenting her with nothing more than a new fabrication. "That's not a fact, that's an outright lie. There was no falling out. We were all getting along fine. I should know. I was there."

"Jenna was there, too. If you don't believe me, maybe you'll believe her."

"You've talked to Jenna about this?"

"I've done better than that." She reached around to unzip the backpack and remove a cell phone. "I've got it all queued up, in Jenna's own words. Would you like to take a listen?"

"Listen to what?"

"It's a recorded session with one of her doctors at the Penn Shepherd Psychiatric Hospital in Dallas."

Ellie gaped at her. "That's private information. There's no legal way you could have obtained such a recording."

"It's one of half a dozen I now have in my possession. How I obtained them is beside the point. Do you want to hear this one or don't you?"

"Why are you doing this?" Ellie asked helplessly.

"Why come to me? If you have information relevant to the kidnapping, then why not go to the local police or to the FBI?"

"Aside from the legalities of the recordings and the need to protect myself, I'm not giving my story away to the cops. Not when I'm so close to solving the case on my own. As for why I'm telling you..." She shrugged. "Believe it or not, I do have a conscience and you need to know what you're up against. Your life could be in danger, too."

Ellie wasn't convinced. "Even if that were true, you don't do anything out of the goodness of your heart."

Melanie smiled. "Maybe you're right. How about an exclusive interview in exchange for what I know?"

"And have you twist my words to justify whatever story you've decided to manufacture? No, thanks. I won't talk to you today or ever. I won't listen to a private recording between Jenna and her doctor. This is a waste of my time."

"And yet you're still here." Melanie held up the phone. "Tell you what. I'll press Play. You can listen or not. Up to you."

Ellie told herself to turn around, march through the gate and not look back. Aside from the fact that Melanie Kent was obviously up to her usual tricks, neither of them had any right to listen to a recorded session between Jenna and her therapist. Ellie could hardly imagine a worse violation of privacy. Yet the moment the recording started to play, she stood paralyzed by something in Jenna's young voice. It was the same subtle quality she'd heard in Hazel Lamont's voice earlier.

An icy breath blew down her collar as she met Melanie Kent's knowing gaze.

How are you feeling today, Jenna?

I'm okay. Tired. I haven't been sleeping well lately. I've been having bad dreams again.

Would you like to talk about them?

I guess.

Whenever you're ready.

(A slight pause.) *It's dark. I'm at the Ruins with Ellie and Riley. I don't want to be there.*

Are you frightened?

No. I don't want to be there because Riley's so mad at me and I have to pretend everything is okay so that Ellie won't get suspicious. What happened is none of her business.

What did happen?

(A longer pause.) *Riley thinks I took something that doesn't belong to me. She came over to my house while I was gone and the housekeeper let her go up to my room.*

She found something of hers in your room?

Some jewelry. I tried to explain that I only wanted to borrow those things, but she wouldn't listen. She started yelling all sorts of hateful accusations at me. I'd never seen her like that. She said she didn't care about most of that stuff, but she wanted her locket back. It belonged to her mother.

You took her mother's locket?

(Defensively.) *In my dream, I took it, but not in real life. I would never do such a thing. You believe me, don't you?*

I believe you, Jenna.

It was such an awful dream. The things she screamed at me. She said if I didn't give her back the locket, she'd tell Ellie's dad that I'd been stealing from her. He'd throw me in jail with all the other criminals.

Ellie's father is the county sheriff, right? In real life and in your dream?

Yes. I've always been a little afraid of him. Most everyone in town is. I knew that if he found out what I'd done, he'd come to my house and arrest me in front of my mom and dad. They'd be so upset. So disappointed in me. I probably wouldn't even be able to finish high school, much less go to college. My whole life would be ruined because of that stupid locket.

Did you give it back to Riley?

Yes. But it didn't change anything. She was still mad at me. She said she didn't want to be my friend anymore. (Resentfully.) *All that fuss over a stupid necklace.*

Why did Riley agree to go out to the Ruins if she was so angry with you?

She didn't want to disappoint Ellie. It was always Ellie this, Ellie that. Honestly, I used to get so tired of the way Riley looked up to her. It wasn't like Ellie was especially nice or even pretty. Sometimes I wanted it to be just the two of us, like it used to be when we were younger. Back in middle school, we did things all the time without Ellie having to horn in.

Is that why you took Riley's things? To get her attention?

(Another long pause.) *You mean in my dream, right?*

(The therapist paused.) *What happened at the Ruins?*

We split up. Ellie went upstairs. She didn't seem to

notice the tension between Riley and me. She never noticed anything that didn't involve her. Riley said she heard a noise. I didn't hear anything but I pretended to go check.

You left Riley alone?

I said I pretended *to go check.*

What happened then, Jenna?

Riley screamed.

Why?

I...don't know.

You don't know why Riley screamed?

Why does it matter? It was just a dream.

A dream that upset you.

Did I say I was upset?

You said you hadn't been sleeping well.

Not because of the dream.

Then what's keeping you awake?

I don't want to talk about this anymore. I'd like to go back to my room now.

In a minute. When you took Riley's locket, did you know that it had belonged to her dead mother?

I knew.

Then you must have also known how much it meant to her. Why did you take it?

Why did I take it in my dream?

Of course.

Because I could.

Chapter Eleven

Sam spotted Ellie on the sidewalk and pulled to the curb, reaching over to push the door open so that she could climb in. She'd put on sunglasses, even though she waited for him in the shade. He couldn't see her eyes, but there was tension around her mouth and in the slight slump of her shoulders.

She closed the door and snapped on her seat belt as he pulled away from the curb. For a moment, neither of them said anything. She stared straight ahead as if her attention were riveted on some distant point. As for Sam, he kept a keen eye on the rearview mirror as he maneuvered through the slow crawl of vehicles around the town square. If a beige sedan lurked somewhere behind him in traffic, he couldn't spot it.

He gave Ellie a sidelong glance. "You okay?"

"I just had an impromptu meeting with Melanie Kent. It's my day for confrontations, it seems."

He glanced at her again, this time in surprise. "Where did this happen?"

"Back in the alley. I think she must have followed

me from the restaurant. She texted, I called her back and we met."

"You met her in an alley?"

"It's smack in the middle of the town square. As she pointed out, I live alone on the lake. If she wanted to hurt me, she could have chosen a much more remote location."

"She said that?" He scowled at the road. "What did she want?"

Ellie turned and met his gaze through the dark glasses. "She claimed to know what really happened to Riley. She said she might even know the location of the remains."

Sam said in astonishment, "Why hasn't she shared that information with the local authorities or the FBI?"

"She said she wants to be the one to solve the case." Her mouth thinned in disgust. "I don't think she has any actual evidence or proof. But she has managed to get her hands on some compelling information for her book."

"What kind of information?"

"Recordings of Jenna's old therapy sessions. She played one for me. She said it was recorded while Jenna was still at Penn Shepherd."

"Are you sure it was the real thing?" Sam asked.

"It sounded authentic. I'd swear it was Jenna's voice. Maybe Melanie paid off an employee of the hospital to duplicate the recordings or hired someone to break into the therapist's office. I don't know. What I do know is that Jenna will be devastated if a transcript of the recording I heard ends up in Melanie's book."

"What was on it?"

"She talked about a disturbing dream she'd had. In this dream, she and Riley were fighting over some missing jewelry. Riley accused Jenna of stealing her mother's locket. She threatened to tell my dad if Jenna didn't return it."

Sam's scowl deepened. "Seems pretty specific for a dream."

"I know. That's why I don't think it was a dream at all. She used the same tactic when she called me last night. I've thought about it a lot. I think pretending she dreamed these things is her way of coping with bad memories."

"You never knew anything about an argument between Riley and Jenna?"

She shook her head. "Maybe Jenna was right. Maybe I was oblivious back then to anything that didn't involve me."

"She said that?"

Ellie shrugged. "She wasn't wrong."

Sam shot her a glance. "Try not to be so hard on yourself. You were fifteen years old."

Ellie sighed. "Seems hard to believe I was ever that young."

Sam observed her out of the corner of his eye. She looked more attractive than usual today in a simple sleeveless dress that complemented her slender waist and subtle curves. Her blond hair was pulled back into a thick straight ponytail and her bare arms and legs against the white dress looked tanned and toned. Her toenails were painted the same pale shade of light pink as her lips. There was nothing provocative or unusual about her clothing or demeanor, and yet Sam found himself thinking that she was one of the most alluring women he'd ever met.

He tapped his fingers impatiently on the steering wheel as he tried to corral his thoughts toward a more neutral direction. "Tell me about Jenna's phone call."

"The one last night?" She nodded. "She talked about the terrible place she and Riley had been taken to. She called it a cell or a cage. It was pitch black. She couldn't locate any windows or doors, just metal bars. She said the floor was cold."

"Did she say anything about the person who had taken them there?"

"No, but she said Riley was really sick. So sick she hadn't eaten or spoken in days."

They exchanged a glance.

"She related all of this as if it were a dream," Ellie said.

While he watched the road, Ellie recounted as much as she could remember of the conversation and how she'd spotted two silhouettes on the dock across the lake that may or may not have been Jenna and Hazel. Then she'd filled him in on the threatening altercation with Hazel at the restaurant.

The phone conversation with Jenna, the confrontation with Hazel and the meeting with Melanie Kent had obviously taken a toll. Ellie seemed more apprehensive and guarded than he'd ever seen her. Her disquiet brought out Sam's protective instincts, though he told himself Ellie Brannon was more than capable of taking care of herself. However, she was right to be cautious.

Things had taken a disturbing turn at the restaurant. Sam knew nothing about Hazel Lamont, but the kind of possessiveness she'd displayed toward Jenna could sometimes spell disaster.

As if reading his mind, Ellie said, "Do you think I should call Jenna's parents? I'm really worried what Hazel might do if she considers them a threat. I'm worried about Jenna, too. If she's fallen under that woman's influence, I shudder to think what might happen."

"You still have their contact information?"

"Yes. I haven't seen or talked to either of them in years and I'm not at all sure they'd even want to hear from me. But I can't sit back and do nothing. Then again, maybe I'm overreacting."

Sam felt her gaze on him. "I still have their information. Why don't I give them a call? Or better yet, maybe I'll go see them in person. Maybe they can shed some light on what's going on with Jenna and Hazel."

Ellie nodded and sat back in her seat. "I really hope I am overreacting but you should have seen the look in her eyes. Her behavior seemed increasingly aggressive. That story she told about an intruder killing her parents and the FBI agent who considered her a suspect..." She hugged her arms around her middle. "I figured she'd made the whole thing up, but now I'm starting to wonder."

"I'll check into it," Sam said. "I know a nurse who used to work at the Penn Shepherd Psychiatric Hospital. We got on pretty well during that time. She was always helpful about getting me in to see Jenna. If she still remembers me, maybe I can get her to open up about Hazel Lamont."

"Ask her about Melanie Kent, too. Maybe she'll have some idea how Melanie got her hands on those recordings." Ellie took off her sunglasses and brushed a hand across her eyes. "You know what else I keep thinking about? Hazel's claim that an older boy had a crush on Riley and the implication that it could have been Cory Small. Riley never said a word to me about an older guy and now it seems unlikely that she would have confided in Jenna. But someone had to have put the notion in Hazel's head."

"Jenna denied she knew anything about a crush."

Ellie seemed to consider the possibilities as she toyed with her sunglasses. "I'm beginning to wonder if I knew either Jenna or Riley as well as I thought I did. Maybe Cory really did have a crush on Riley and, for whatever reason, she felt she couldn't tell me. Sam—" She caught herself and offered a quick apology. "Sorry. Agent Reece."

He said easily, "Sam is fine."

She gave him a reluctant glance. "I don't know that I'm ready to be on a first-name basis with you. Maybe we should keep things a little more formal."

Her eyes looked translucent in the sunlight shining in through the windshield, her lips lush and glistening. He wondered what it would be like to kiss those lips and abruptly turned his attention back to the road. "I don't see a problem. We've known each other for a long time."

"That's not really true. You know everything there

is to know about me, but I know hardly anything about you. Maybe that's for the best."

Sam lifted a hand and rubbed the back of his neck. "Whatever makes you more comfortable." He felt unaccountably disappointed, which only served to prove her point. "Let's talk a little more about Cory Small."

She said in relief, "Okay, but I've already told you everything I remember about him. I never really knew him, even though our school was fairly small. He was older so we didn't run in the same circles. I'm not even sure I would recognize him if I met him on the street." She paused. "You don't think he had anything to do with the kidnapping, do you? My dad looked into him because of his relationship to Silas Creed. If Dad had thought there was anything suspicious about him or his mother, he would have come down hard on both of them."

"I checked him out, too," Sam said. "He had an alibi for the night in question and we never found any physical evidence that linked him or his mother to the kidnapping. When I talked to him yesterday, he swore neither of them had heard from Creed since he left town fifteen years ago."

"Of course he'd say that."

"True." Sam turned onto the highway and headed toward the lake. The road behind them remained clear. "Something interesting happened while I was out at that farm." He shot another glance in the rearview before glancing at Ellie. "I mentioned earlier that Melanie Kent is staying in a converted garden shed to write her book. That shed is at the back of Cory Small's property.

It's the same one Silas Creed used to hole up in when things got tense for him in town."

Ellie had been gazing out the window but now she whirled to face him. "Is that where you found the pictures of Jenna and me?"

"Yes. Did you ask Melanie about those photographs?"

"I didn't even think about it," Ellie admitted. "Maybe that's a good thing because I'm guessing she doesn't know you went through her things. But it does make my blood run cold, the idea of her skulking around, taking pictures of us without our knowing. At least I know now to keep an eye out for her."

"There's something else you need to know," Sam said. "I saw a hat hanging on the wall in the nursery. Black. Wide-brimmed." He glanced at Ellie. She sat rapt.

"Cory said the hat had belonged to his mother. Apparently, it went missing a couple of days ago. Then it reappeared in the greenhouse yesterday, which means it would have been gone from its usual place at the same time you spotted someone in a black hat by the lake. Cory seemed to think Melanie took it."

"I wish I could say that I'm surprised, but I'm not," Ellie said. "I suspected even before we talked today that Melanie Kent was somehow involved in everything that's happened. But what could she hope to accomplish by pretending to be Preacher? I have no doubt she'd do anything for a story, but what's she really after?"

"Maybe it's something as simple as her wanting to get a rise out of you. Force you into making a statement she can quote in her book. Or maybe it's some kind of publicity stunt. I'll drive back out there later and see if I can get her to talk to me. She's one cool cookie, but an FBI badge has a way of shaking people up."

Ellie nodded. "Do you think she planted the idea in Hazel's head about Riley and Cory Small? Maybe she heard something on one of the tapes."

"It's possible, but I'm inclined to think it was the other way around. Maybe Hazel planted that seed in Melanie's head."

"Why would she do that?"

"I can think of one reason." He turned to meet her gaze. "Maybe she's setting Cory up as a scapegoat."

"For what?"

"You and Jenna and Riley were best friends. Closer than sisters, you said. Riley's gone, but you're still here. Maybe Hazel thinks of you as a rival."

"But Jenna and I hardly ever see each other anymore."

"You're still an important part of her life. She thinks about you, talks about you. In Hazel's mind, you're someone who could take Jenna away from her."

Ellie's eyes widened as the implication sank in. "My God. Are you saying she might try to harm me?"

"It's a theory," he said. "It explains everything that's happened—the anonymous calls from someone pretending to be Riley. Maybe she was the one in that black hat pretending to be Preacher. What better way to keep you frightened and off balance?"

"How does Melanie Kent figure into all this?"

"I suspect Hazel is using her in some way. I haven't

put it all together yet, but I'm starting to see how some of the pieces may fit. I need to get back to Dallas as soon as possible."

"Should we go back for my car, then?"

"I don't mean today, but soon." He resisted the urge to put his hand over Ellie's to reassure her. "I'm not trying to scare you, but until we know more about Hazel Lamont, it's best to keep your distance. Probably a good idea to stay away from Melanie Kent, too, while you're at it."

I'M NOT TRYING to scare you...

Too late, Ellie thought as she folded her arms and shivered. Aloud she said, "You need to take the next left and then a hard right. The bridge is only a quarter of a mile or so from the turnoff."

Sam followed her directions without comment. He'd gone silent after his warning about Hazel and Melanie. Maybe he regretted his candid speculation. It all seemed so farfetched when spoken aloud, but then, Hazel was right. Ellie had never dealt with anyone like her. The woman seemed clever and cunning and she'd all but threatened Ellie back at the restaurant. What if she really did view Ellie as a rival for Jenna's friendship and affection? Was she using Melanie Kent's ruthless ambition to set up Cory Small to be the fall guy for Ellie's elimination?

Ellie stared out the window, but the beauty of the countryside barely registered. Fifteen years after the kidnapping, she found herself once again drowning in fear and uncertainty. Would she ever be free of this nightmare?

"You okay?"

She answered without turning. "Sometimes I wonder if it will ever be over."

"I wonder that, too, at times."

"It always comes back to that night. The decisions we made. How different so many lives would be today if we hadn't gone out to the Ruins."

"It does no good to look back," Sam said. "All any of us can do is try to navigate the here and now."

She pointed to the turnoff. "Speaking of which… that way."

He pulled onto the narrow lane and the shade from the encroaching woods stretched over the car. Ellie lowered her window and the fecund scent of the swamp drifted in, conjuring images of dark water and deep secrets. They rounded the final bend and the cabin came into view, a modest A-frame perched on stilts with wide decks and sweeping views of the lake.

The tires crunched on the gravel drive as Sam pulled to a stop. He sat for a moment, taking in their surroundings before turning to Ellie. "Who owns this place?"

"His name was Charles Nance. He was murdered earlier in the summer. It was in all the local papers. If you've kept tabs on the community, I'm sure you heard about it."

"The doctor, right? That was a big case for the county sheriff's office."

"I doubt Tom looks at it that way. Dr. Nance's death

was a blow to all of us. The cabin has sat empty since his passing."

"Maybe we should knock on the door anyway just in case."

They got out of the car together and walked up the porch steps. Sam glanced at Ellie as he knocked. When no one answered, he peered through the sidelights. "Place looks deserted. Let's check around back."

They took a quick perusal of the back deck and then descended the wooden steps to the dock. Ellie stood at the very edge, letting her gaze drift along the opposite bank. She couldn't help catching glimpses of Sam out of the corner of her eye. He'd changed into jeans and a plain gray T-shirt back at the inn. He looked the same and yet completely different without his formal FBI attire. The slight shimmer at his temples mesmerized her before she forced her attention back to the distant bank.

"The Thayer house is directly across the lake," she said.

"That's where you feed the peacocks?"

"Peafowl. Male and female. And yes, that's also where I saw someone in a black hat. He stood at the top of that embankment. I assumed it was a man at the time, but now you've made me think the person may have been Melanie or Hazel. I never got a look at the face." She pointed out her house and studio. "You can see the broadcast tower through the pine trees. That's my bedroom window. I was looking out at the lake when I saw Jenna and Hazel here on this dock. I still can't figure out why they'd come out here in the middle of the night. Hazel, sure, if she's behind everything. But

Jenna? I don't want to believe she has anything to do with this."

"She may not be the person you've always thought her to be," Sam said.

"I know. And I can't discount Hazel's influence, either. It's possible she's convinced Jenna I'm to blame for what happened to her. Jenna seemed so bitter and resentful at lunch."

"Try to keep it in perspective. Whatever else is going on with Jenna, she's lived through a horror that few people can imagine. Good or bad, she'll never be the person she was before the kidnapping."

They stood in deep shade at the end of the dock. Sam took off his sunglasses and slipped them in his pocket. His eyes were dark and intense as he stared down at her. "We'll figure this out together."

"You sound so sure, but it's been fifteen years since Riley went missing."

"Something's changed," Sam said.

Between them, too. It wasn't just the fact that his given name had slipped through her lips so easily or the way his eyes darkened to navy when he stared down at her. Ellie didn't want to contemplate her attraction on any deep level, but all of a sudden her awareness of Sam Reece was all she could think about.

"It's strange, isn't it?" she said.

"What is?"

"When we first met, I found you intimidating. You seemed so cold and single-minded and I resented all your questions. I hated you for making me relive that terrible night over and over."

"And now?"

"Here we are fifteen years later working together to figure things out." She glanced up at him. "I'll do whatever I can to help you."

"You'll go back to the Ruins with me?"

"Yes. I doubt my memory will be jolted after all this time, but I suppose we have to try." Her gaze lifted reluctantly to the smokestack rising up through the treetops. "Did you know that you can see it from here?"

He turned, following her gaze. "The smokestack? I'm surprised it's even still standing. It's a wonder someone hasn't bulldozed that whole place to the ground by now."

"I've thought about that hospital so often. Dreamed about it hundreds of times. I still go over everything in my mind, trying to figure out what I might have seen, what I might have missed that night."

"You were attacked from behind. Maybe you really didn't see anything," Sam said.

"I remember the rag over my face and the fumes. I wouldn't have gone under immediately. We must have struggled. I must have fought him. Yet I never caught a glimpse of his face."

"He was careful," Sam said. "It's possible he wore a mask. We know he must have had everything planned out in advance."

"Does that sound like something Silas Creed could do?"

"You said yourself, he was an educated man. He could have gotten his hands on chloroform from any number of sources or he could have made his own with bleach and acetone. As to the timing, he was known to hang out around local schools and playgrounds. He spied on people through their windows. He could have overheard some of your classmates talking about the dare."

"Do you really believe that?"

Sam hesitated. "I've always had my doubts he acted alone, but it's possible." He moved to the other side of the dock and stared out over the water. "We'll go after dark."

Ellie's heart lurched. "Tonight?"

"Better to get it over with. I'll drive back to Dallas first thing in the morning."

Uncertainty crept over her. "What if I don't remember anything? What if we go through that awful place and nothing comes back to me?"

"Then you'll have at least proved to yourself that you can stare down the monsters."

Chapter Twelve

After Ellie picked up her car in town, Sam followed her back out to the lake. She fixed sandwiches and iced tea for a late lunch and they ate on the deck with a soft breeze drifting off the water. Later, they walked over to the Thayer house to feed the peafowl and then they returned to the deck to watch the sunset. The breeze cooled as the light faded. Ellie went inside to change into shorts and sneakers and grab a flashlight.

Sam waited for her on the dock. He stood at the railing, peering into the water as she approached. The platform rocked slightly as she moved up beside him. With the coming darkness, her dread had blossomed. She tried not to think about what lay ahead. Tried not to panic when she contemplated the moment she stepped through that crumbling doorway.

"If you lean far enough over the water, you can see the smokestack from here, as well," she said. "Urban legend had it that the boiler room was also used as a crematorium. I doubt that's true. But there is a tunnel that leads from the basement out to the boiler room. I never learned the purpose of that tunnel."

"I've been through it," Sam said. "We searched every inch of that building after the kidnapping. I went out there a couple of times by myself. Creepy place even in daylight."

"Did you ever find anything?"

"Nothing useful."

"I've never been particularly superstitious, but that place..." She trailed off on a shiver. "Looking back, I'm not sure how we mustered the courage to go inside."

"Kids do all sorts of things on a dare," Sam said.

She turned back to the water. "When should we go?"

"Let's wait for the moon to rise. As I said, I'd like to see the place from your perspective that night."

"Sam—" She didn't correct herself this time.

He straightened and turned, his eyes glinting in the dark. He looked tall and fit and steady. Reassuring.

His gaze on her intensified. "What is it?"

"Do you really think this is a good idea?"

"Yes. Don't you?"

"I thought so earlier when the sun was shining. Now I don't know." She glanced down into those obsidian depths. The water lilies had closed for the night and the bullfrogs were just tuning up. It was a beautiful setting, lonely and primal. Ellie suppressed another shiver as she leaned over the railing and traced the smokestack silhouetted against the rising moon. "We should probably go before I change my mind."

But they waited until the moon soared over the treetops and then they left the dock to follow the trail along the bank. As they neared the bridge, Ellie paused and angled her flashlight beam up under the braces.

"We left our bikes here that night. We covered them with leaves and branches so they couldn't be spotted from the bridge."

"You rode all the way out here from town?"

"It's only a few miles." She shrugged. "We were young. I remember we barely spoke the whole way. After we'd hidden the bikes, we used our flashlights to find the trail. By that time, the eclipse was almost over, but the moon still had a bloody hue. Riley said it was a sign that we shouldn't go on, but I told her we'd come too far to turn back. I suggested she wait for us at the bridge if she was too afraid, but Jenna said we should all stick together. It was safer in numbers." Ellie thought back to Jenna's voice on the tape. *I don't want to be there because Riley's so mad at me and I have to pretend everything is okay so that Ellie won't get suspicious.*

She moved back to the path and Sam fell in beside her.

"People say this lake is haunted. On a clear night when the moon is up and the wind is still, you can hear the echo of screams across the water. Screams from the lost souls trapped in the Ruins and from the Native Americans that were forced from their land by settlers. That's why they call it Echo Lake."

"Have you ever heard the screams?" he asked.

"Yes, from the peacocks."

As if on cue, a staccato cry echoed out over the water. *Uhhhhh. Uhhhhh. Uhhhhh. Uhhhhh.*

The sound undulated down through the trees, stopping Sam dead in his tracks. "Good Lord. *That* was a peacock?"

"You've never heard one before?"

"I think I would have remembered that scream. It's inhuman and yet uncannily human at the same time. Like a child in terrible pain."

"The stuff of nightmares and legends," Ellie said.

Sam swore as he glanced out over the water. Then he turned back to the path. "Let's keep going."

But something had changed during that interlude. They both grew tense as they neared the Ruins. Ellie lingered on the path to run her flashlight beam up the steep embankment.

"Doesn't look too bad," Sam said.

They used vines and tree roots to pull themselves toward the summit where they paused yet again as the Ruins loomed before them, a three-story mausoleum with arched windows and doors that must once have been beautiful. Moonlight glinted off jagged glass, creating the illusion of watchful eyes. Ivy and trumpet vines crept up the side of the building, snaking through broken windows and over the caved-in roof.

The place seemed alive, as if decades of memories and misery had somehow been personified in those crumbling walls. Ellie was almost afraid to speak, so powerful was the spell. A breeze drifted through the trees, sounding for the world like the whispers of all those trapped souls.

She closed her eyes on a shudder. "This is as far as I've come since that night."

Sam's gaze raked over the walls. "I'd forgotten how

imposing this place is, especially in the dark. And yet there's something almost stately about the remains."

The remains. What an apt choice of words, Ellie thought. "Should we go inside now?"

"Tell me what you did fifteen years ago."

"We huddled outside for a bit. As you said, it's an imposing sight. I remember the way Riley clutched my arm as we gazed up at all those broken windows."

"What about Jenna?"

"She stood on the other side of Riley. A little away from us now that I think about it, but maybe that recording has colored my memory. I remember she was very protective of Riley. She kept asking if she wanted to turn back. Eventually, we walked through the weeds to the front steps. I remember thinking about snakes. It was summer and the copperheads and moccasins were out."

Sam shone his flashlight beam across the overgrown grounds to the front steps. "I'll lead the way—scare off any reptiles in our path."

"No, let me. I went first that night."

Sam stepped aside and she moved past him on the path, her insides tingling with fear and excitement as she brushed against his arm. He felt warm and stable, a sentient reassurance in that withering place.

Her sneakers whispered against the concrete as she climbed the steps and hovered at the threshold. She said over her shoulder, "I went in first, then Riley and Jenna. I remember thinking as I stepped through the door that maybe our coming out here hadn't been such a good idea after all. The place felt cold to me. Haunted.

I didn't believe in ghosts. I still don't. And yet…" She glanced back to make sure Sam was behind her.

"I felt it the first time I came here," he said. "I've felt it in other places, too, where children have gone missing. Like a lingering evil."

Ellie's voice dropped to a whisper. "Did you have to say that?"

He flicked the beam past her into the interior. "Watch your step."

They made their way through the lobby, the floorboards creaking beneath their shoes. The dueling beams of their flashlights arced over the walls, into the shadowy corners and finally up to the ceiling where Preacher's red eyes gleamed beneath the brim of his black hat.

Ellie gasped. "My God. I had no idea the painting was so large."

"This is the first time I've seen it, too," Sam said.

"The local paper did a story on it years ago. They ran photographs. I thought I knew what to expect…" Those red eyes seemed to mesmerize Ellie so that she had to tear her gaze away. "No one knows who painted it. It just seemed to appear one day. People trekked out here for months to stare up at it and take pictures."

"But not you."

"No, not me. I tell myself it's just graffiti painted on the ceiling of an old building."

"Where to now?" Sam asked.

They were at the bottom of the stairs. "This is where we separated. I went up to the second floor and Jenna stayed here with Riley. She begged me not to go and

Jenna insisted again that we should all stick together. I wanted to prove how brave I was. I told Riley not to be a baby. That was the last thing I ever said to her."

"You couldn't have known what would happen."

"Maybe I should have known. There must have been some clue we weren't alone. A closing door, a creaking floorboard. Something. But I don't remember anything out of the ordinary."

"Let's go up to the second floor and take a look."

"I need to go up there alone," Ellie said.

"I don't think that's necessary. Just being here in the dark is enough to trigger a memory. Besides, we've no way of knowing the condition of the floors up there, let alone the staircase."

"I'll be careful. I need to do this alone."

Sam ran his beam up the curving staircase, trailing it along the wrought iron banister that hung loose in places. "I don't like this. That's a steep staircase. If you fall through, you could break a leg or worse."

"This was your idea, remember? I'll be fine. If I need you, I'll call out. Otherwise, I'll do exactly as I did that night."

She went up the stairs slowly, chasing away shadows with her flashlight. She paused at the top to glance back down at Sam. He stood in almost the exact same spot where she'd last seen Riley. Ellie had hesitated on the landing that night, staring down at her friends as she secretly bolstered her courage.

Willing the memories to come, she eased across the landing and started down the corridor. The old elevator shaft was somewhere ahead, a gaping hole that dropped all the way to the basement.

"Everything okay?"

Sam's voice echoed up the stairwell. Ellie had the strongest urge to rush back down the steps, straight into his arms, but instead she cleared her throat and called back to him. "I'm fine. I'd only been up here a few minutes that night when I heard a scream."

"Which one of the girls screamed?"

"I was never certain." She closed her eyes, remembering Jenna's voice on the recording. "I think it was Riley."

"Is that a memory?"

"I don't know."

"Pretend you just heard the scream. What did you do then?"

"I turned and rushed back to the landing. I peered over the banister before I started down the stairs."

"Do that now."

She turned back, the flashlight beam arching over the walls and down into the empty corridor. For a moment, Ellie could have sworn she saw someone lurking in the shadows. A black-clad figure with a hat pulled low over his eyes.

Her imagination. She was merely projecting into the shadows what she had glimpsed on the ceiling. Preacher was dead. *Dead.*

The shadow moved. For a moment, Ellie stood frozen, unable to call out, unable to breathe.

"Ellie? You okay?"

"Sam—Sam!"

The shadow rushed toward her. Ellie screamed and whirled, dashing headlong toward the stairs, forgetting about rotting floorboards and dangerous stairwells. She was nearly at the landing when the phantom caught up with her. He grabbed her from behind and pushed her hard against the banister. Rusted bolts snapped and a section of the wrought iron swung away from the wall, carrying Ellie with it. She dangled in midair as she imagined herself falling through the floorboards below all the way down into the basement.

Dimly, she heard Sam call her name and the sound of his footsteps clamoring up the stairs. Another bolt snapped and the railing dropped several inches. Ellie's fingers slipped as the jagged metal ate into her flesh.

Sam was on the landing by this time. He placed the flashlight on the floor and reached for Ellie, but the railing had swung just out of his grasp.

He thrust his hand toward her. "Grab hold of my fingers. I'll pull you toward me."

"I can't."

"It's okay. I won't let you fall."

She flailed, missed his hand, and the railing creaked and shuddered as she swayed.

"Again," he said.

She tried to inch closer, but with every movement, the banister gave a little more. Sam was on his stomach now, hanging over the edge of the landing as he reached for the banister, swinging her toward him, grabbing her wrist, pulling her to safety just as the last bolt gave way and the heavy wrought iron crashed to the floor.

Ellie lay shaking for a moment before she scrambled

away from the edge. Sam followed her. She pulled her legs up and hugged her knees as she pressed her back against the wall.

"Someone was up here," she said. "Did you see him?"

He shook his head slowly. "I saw you go through the banister. I thought you must have tripped."

"I didn't trip. I was pushed."

"Did you see who it was?"

"Yes." She clutched Sam's hand as her voice lowered to a whisper. "It was Preacher."

SAM HUNKERED BESIDE her on the landing. "What?"

Her grasp tightened. "You have to go after him! Don't let him get away!"

"Hold on. What did you actually see?"

"Someone in a black hat. I think he had a mask over his face."

"You're sure it was a man?"

"I don't know!" She tried to scramble to her feet, but he held her in place.

"Did he have a weapon?"

"Not that I saw—"

She broke off as Sam's head came up. He put a fingertip to his lips to silence her. Then he drew his weapon and swiveled toward the corridor. He peered through the shadows before lifting his gaze to the ceiling. Someone was on the third floor directly above them.

He pressed his finger to his lips again and then pointed skyward. Ellie tipped her head, tracking the soft footsteps. "He's up there," she whispered.

Sam put his lips close to her ear. “He’s trying to find a way out. Wait here.”

When he would have stood, she pulled him back down. “Be careful. This isn’t a hoax.”

He nodded and rose, then moved quickly and quietly down the corridor, flashlight positioned over his weapon. He swept the beam through the empty rooms as he went, making sure an accomplice didn’t still lurk on the second floor.

Every now and then, he stopped to listen. The footsteps had gone silent. He didn’t think the suspect had had time to climb out a window, much less scale down a wall. More likely he’d found a hiding place—

Sam froze, one foot poised over nothing but air. He hovered on the brink of the old elevator shaft for a heart-stopping moment before he managed to regain his balance. Then he trained the beam down into the pitch-black chute, almost expecting to see gleaming eyes staring back up at him.

Sidestepping the shaft, he eased down the corridor until the sound of breaking glass halted him at the bottom of another stairwell. He turned off the flashlight and tucked it into the back of his jeans. Using both hands to steady his weapon, he went up the steps and flattened himself against the wall of the landing.

Moonlight filtered in through the long windows at the end of the corridor and through the gaping holes in the roof. A rat scurried across his shoe as he stood listening. Weapon at the ready, he started down the corridor, moving past one room after another before he backtracked to a doorway where shards of glass glittered on the floor. Most of the windows in the building were either broken out or boarded up. The unsub must have knocked out the jagged glass so that he could safely crawl through.

Sam tried to step quietly, but his boots crunched on the shards as he moved to the window and leaned out. The night wind blew across his face as he trailed his gaze down the wall.

Out of the corner of his eye, he caught a quick movement on the narrow ledge that ran the length of the building just beneath the windows. Someone in a black hoodie stood flattened against the wall. He seemed to be searching for a way down. When he saw Sam, he sprinted around the corner.

Putting away his weapon, Sam crawled out the window and paused to get his footing as he glanced down three stories to the ground. He pressed his back to the wall and closed his eyes briefly. He'd never much cared for heights.

Inching sideways, he kept his back to the wall, pausing to peer around the corner where the assailant had disappeared. The ledge was empty.

Sam glanced downward. He saw nothing, heard nothing. It was as if the unsub had disappeared into thin air.

Then he spotted an old metal ladder bolted to the wall that went up to the roof. It must have been once used for maintenance. Sam went up quickly, pretending a three-story fall wouldn't break every bone in his body. Hitching himself up over the eaves, he scrambled crab-like up to the peak and cautiously straightened to survey his surroundings. From this vantage, the building looked much larger than from the inside. Many of the shingles had long since crumbled away, exposing large sections of rotted wood.

Halfway along the peak, a black-clad figure stood silhouetted against the full moon.

Sam called out to the suspect. "Federal agent! Stop where you are!"

The figure glanced over his shoulder as he moved erratically along the peak, seemingly driven by panic. Sam lunged after him, gaining confidence as he picked up speed.

"Federal Agent! I said stop!"

Cornered, the figure glanced around frantically and then half scrambling, half sliding, he went back down the slope, positioning himself at the very edge as he contemplated his predicament.

Sam pulled his weapon. "Hands up!"

The suspect teetered at the edge before he went over. For a dizzying second, Sam thought he had jumped. He scrambled down the slope and peered over the edge. The suspect had somehow managed to cling to an old drain-pipe. He shimmied down to the ledge and then used the tangle of vines to rappel to the ground.

As Sam stood watching, the suspect landed with a thud and sprinted for the woods.

Chapter Thirteen

A little while later, Sam sat on a barstool in Ellie's kitchen and watched as she rummaged frantically through her cabinets. Neither of them had said much on the way home, but it was obvious the adrenaline was still pumping.

"What are you looking for?" he finally asked.

"I know I've got a bottle of whiskey around here somewhere. Aha!" She produced a nearly full bottle and got down two shot glasses, filling both to the rim.

Sam picked up his glass. "You sure you want to do this?"

"Yes. My nerves are still a mess." She eyed him over the rim before she downed the contents. "I still say you should have shot him. Her. Whoever."

"The Bureau frowns on shooting unarmed suspects in the back."

"He tried to kill me."

"I know," Sam said grimly. He chugged the whiskey.

Ellie tried to replenish his glass but he held up a hand blocking her. "That's it for me. Best to keep a clear head for the rest of the night."

"Fine." She poured herself another drink and tossed it back. The fire seemed to momentarily take her breath away. She took a deep breath and shuddered. "Okay. I'm done."

"Should we call your brother?"

She scowled. "Why? Whoever was behind that mask is long gone. There's nothing Tom or anyone else can do tonight."

"You're going to have to tell him at some point. He needs to know what's going on in his county, much less with his sister."

"I know that. Of course, I'll eventually tell him, but it's your case, right? The FBI is in charge."

"I doubt he would agree with that assessment. Is there some reason you don't want him to know?"

"Aside from the fact that he worries too much? It's not so much Tom I'm keeping in the dark as it is his fiancée, Rae. Rae Cavanaugh. Riley's sister."

"You mentioned they were engaged."

Her eyes glittered from the whiskey. "Since you've kept abreast of everything going on in Bell Pointe I assume you know about Rae's niece."

"She was kidnapped and held for ransom," he said.

Ellie nodded. "You can't imagine all the bad memories that were stirred for that family, especially Rae. She had to relive her worst nightmare. And then to find out about her brother..." Ellie trailed away. "She finally has something good in her life. Something to celebrate. I don't want to be the one to take that away from her."

"You've done nothing wrong," he said reasonably.

"I know, but can't we just give them a little more

time? At least until morning. There really isn't anything Tom can do tonight except worry." She eyed the whiskey bottle for a moment and then returned it to the cabinet. "You know what I can't figure out? How that person knew you and I would be at the Ruins tonight. The attack can't have been random nor could we have been followed. That person was already hiding out on the second floor when we arrived."

"I've been thinking about that, too," Sam said. "Come outside with me."

"No, thank you. I'd rather stay right here behind locked doors if you don't mind."

"This will only take a minute."

They went out to the deck. The moon was still up, casting an eerie glow over the preternatural landscape. Ellie's face looked pale and drawn. She was putting up a good front, but the attack at the Ruins had left her shaken. It had left Sam rattled, too. He didn't want to think what would have happened if he hadn't been able to pull her up in time. Maybe she would have walked away from a one-story fall. Then again, people had died from tumbling off ladders.

"What are we doing out here?" Ellie asked with a shiver.

"Wait here." Sam went down the steps and angled his beam under the deck where Ellie stored lawn equipment and old patio furniture. Then he shined the light up through floorboards.

Ellie called down to him. "What are you doing down there?"

He came back up the steps. "Someone could have

hidden under your deck and listened to every word we said earlier. All they had to do was slip away, hide in the Ruins and wait for us to come."

Ellie shivered. "Hazel did threaten me earlier."

"It may have been Hazel, but anyone could have followed us out here from town." He shined the light down through the floorboards.

Ellie cast a wary glance toward the lake. "She could still be around, sitting in a boat somewhere, watching us. The shadows on the other side of the bank are so thick, we'd never see her."

"Let's not get ahead of ourselves. We don't know that it was Hazel."

"We don't really know anything." She turned to go back inside, waiting for Sam to follow so that she could close and lock the door. "What do we do now?"

"I don't want to leave you alone tonight. I'll bunk down here on the couch."

"I appreciate that, but you don't need to sleep on the couch. I have a spare room down the hallway. The bathroom is stocked with whatever you need. Sometimes a guest will stay over after a live interview so I make sure to keep a fresh toothbrush around."

"Thanks. I'll be fine."

She hesitated at the bottom of the stairs. "This is getting stranger and stranger. Even for my world."

"And for mine," he said. "But we will figure it out."

"So you keep saying."

After Ellie had gone upstairs, Sam walked from room to room, familiarizing himself with the layout of the house. He checked all the doors and then stood guard at the windows overlooking the deck. The night was still. Almost too still. He could hear Ellie moving around upstairs and desire stirred as his imagination kicked in.

He told himself it was just the residual adrenaline, but deep down he knew better. He'd allowed Ellie Brannon to get under his skin. Not a good time for distractions when a fifteen-year-old investigation was just starting to heat up.

ELLIE LAY ON her back and stared up at the ceiling, hoping the shifting patterns would eventually lull her to sleep. No such luck. Even the whiskey had failed to settle her nerves. She went back over everything that had happened at the Ruins, getting herself so worked up that she tossed the covers aside and rose, padding over to the window to stare out at the moonlit lake.

She felt anxious and wired and braced herself for that paralyzing moment when panic engulfed her. It didn't come. Maybe that was a sign. Maybe something good had come out of that trip to the Ruins. After fifteen years of nightmares, maybe she'd finally faced down her monsters.

Or maybe they'd just gone into hiding.

She searched the shadows for a moment and then moved her gaze back to the lake. The water shimmered like fine silk in the moonlight. She pushed up the window and leaned into the night.

Footsteps sounded on the stairs. She turned as Sam appeared in the doorway. He'd taken off his shirt and shoes. His jeans hung low on his hips. Ellie's breath caught. She'd never seen anything so startlingly sexy as Sam Reece standing in her bedroom doorway.

"You okay? I heard a noise," he said.

His deep voice tripped along her nerve endings. "I opened the window," she said. "I needed some fresh air."

He glanced toward the rumpled bed. "Couldn't sleep?"

"I'm still too keyed up." She turned back to the window. "Come take a look at the view."

He moved up beside her.

"My brother hates that I live out here alone, but this is why I stay." She breathed in the fragrant air. "Have you ever seen anything so beautiful?"

She felt his gaze on her. "No," he said. "I don't think I have."

They weren't touching and yet Ellie's skin tingled as if he'd run his fingers down her arm. She glanced up at him. His eyes were as dark and shimmery as the moonlit lake. Tension crackled for the longest moment and then she leaned into him, cupping his face as she stood on tiptoes to kiss him.

He leaned back slightly. "Are you sure about this?"

She responded by bringing his lips down to hers. He wrapped his arms around her, lifting her off the floor as he kissed her back. He lowered her slowly and then they silently undressed in the moonlight. Ellie crawled back into bed and he slid in beside her. Arms and legs entwined, their kisses grew more heated until Ellie gently pushed him away.

He rolled to his side and propped himself up on his elbow. "Should I go back downstairs?"

"I don't want you to leave. I just want to slow things down a bit."

"Okay."

"Tell me something about yourself. Something personal so that I feel I know you."

He wound a strand of her hair around his fingertip. "What do you want to know?"

"Where did you grow up? Where did you go to school?"

"Longview. My parents and sister still live there. I went to school at UT Austin. The FBI recruited during my senior year." He rolled to his back and stared up at the ceiling. "I was near the top of my class at Quantico so I expected an assignment at headquarters, or possibly a field office in New York or LA. Instead, I was sent to the satellite office in Tyler, Texas. The kiss of death before my career had ever gotten off the ground."

"Why?"

"Who knows? Maybe I pissed off someone important or maybe I impressed myself more than I did the powers-that-be. Looking back, it was probably a deserved comeuppance. I was a little too full of myself. I can see that now, but at the time, I was devastated. Which is why I pushed so hard when I was assigned to Riley's kidnapping. I should have concentrated more on solving the case than on proving my brilliance."

"You did all you could. My father was an excellent lawman. He couldn't solve the case, either."

"Eventually I was sent back to DC where I was assigned to one of the Child Abduction Rapid Deployment teams. I had a lot to learn."

"You've hunted monsters ever since," she said. "It's a noble job but it must take a toll."

"You find ways to cope."

"Never been married?"

"No."

"Engaged?"

"No. Relationships are hard in my profession."

"I can only imagine."

"What about you?" He turned, lifting himself on his elbow again as he stared down at her.

"No husbands, no fiancés, no boyfriend at the moment. Relationships are hard for me, too. Trust is an issue."

"I can only imagine."

"I like sex, though."

He bent and kissed her neck. "Good to know."

She slid her hand under the covers. Sam's breath sharpened. He fell back against the pillows, succumbing to the cleverness of her fingers before he rolled on top of her. Bracing his hands on either side of her, he stared deep into her eyes. A smile tugged as he brought his lips to hers, tasting her with his tongue and then sliding slowly downward. He touched and teased until Ellie clutched the covers and twisted her fingers in his hair. When he finally came up for air, she was breathing hard and tingling all over.

She reached inside the nightstand drawer. Her gaze raked over the pistol, but that wasn't the protection she sought. She found the packet, tore it open and dealt efficiently with the contents.

Sam shuddered as she touched him. She climbed on top of him, pushing back her hair as she positioned her hips. Moonlight pooled over their naked bodies as she moved, slowly at first and then with feverish abandon. Maybe it was the adrenaline, maybe it was the whiskey, more than likely it was Sam Reece himself. His dark eyes drew her in as his deep whispers egged her on until she collapsed, shuddering against his chest.

Chapter Fourteen

Sam left for Dallas at midmorning, but not before he'd surprised Ellie with breakfast on the deck and extracted a promise that she would call Tom sometime that day to fill him in on recent events. She walked him out to the car and they kissed goodbye, a perfectly natural and affectionate gesture without any of the awkwardness Ellie had been dreading.

She watched until his car disappeared down the road and then she went back inside to work. Settling down in her office with a fresh cup of coffee, she went over the previous notes she'd made for a remote interview she would be recording later that afternoon for a future broadcast. She was thankful to have a pressing assignment to keep her thoughts occupied.

Breaking for a late lunch, she texted Sam to make sure he'd arrived safely in Dallas, to which he promptly responded, and then she decided to give her brother a call.

To her surprise, a woman answered Tom's cell phone.

"Rae? Did I call the wrong number?"

"Not if you're trying to reach Tom," her future sister-in-law responded. "Is everything okay?"

"I was about to ask you the same thing."

Rae sighed. "Everything's fine, but your brother is being as stubborn as always. He refuses to accept the fact that he's not yet one hundred percent. His doctor and I have both warned him about overdoing it. A gunshot wound doesn't heal overnight, or even over the course of a few months. I insisted he take the day off. He's only allowed to respond to emergencies." She paused. "Do I sound as much like a nag as I think I do?"

"You sound like you're looking out for my brother. He is okay, isn't he?" Ellie asked anxiously.

"He's fine. To be honest, I mostly wanted a day to ourselves so we can go over our wedding plans together. But if you need him, I can go get him."

"No," Ellie said quickly. "It's nothing that can't wait. I'll call him back in a day or two. Don't even bother telling him that I called."

They spoke for a minute or two longer and then Ellie went back to work. Just before four that afternoon, she gathered up her notes and a copy of her guest's latest book and headed over to the studio. Sunlight shimmered down through the pine bowers, but on the opposite bank, shadows had already started to lengthen. She peered through the trees, wondering if someone watched from across the water. Or from somewhere even closer.

Maybe she should have asked Tom to send a patrol car by now and then. She hated asking for special favors. It put her brother in an awkward position. Besides,

Sam would be back soon and she'd equipped the studio with strong locks to protect her expensive equipment. She'd be fine.

Once inside, she bolted the door and seated herself behind her console, positioning her chair so that she could see out the large window. She was safer here in her soundproof studio than almost anywhere else in the world.

Or so she wanted to believe.

SAM GLANCED AT his watch. Ellie would be in the studio by now. She'd likely turned off her cell for the interview so he had no way of getting in touch with her. He sent a text anyway, alerting her that he would be returning later than he'd originally planned. Jenna's parents had agreed to meet with him, but not until after church and a potluck luncheon that had been on their schedule for months.

He located the address and pulled to the curb in front of the one-story ranch, a much more modest home than the stately Victorian he remembered from his previous time in Belle Pointe. Jenna's treatments in expensive facilities like the Penn Shepherd Psychiatric Hospital had undoubtedly taken a toll on their finances.

Glancing over his shoulder, he walked up the porch steps and rang the bell. Both of the Malloys greeted him at the door. They'd been in their mid-forties when Jenna had been taken and then later found wandering along a country road. They would be approaching sixty now and the passing years of despair and heartache were deeply etched into their faces. They were both tall and slender, still an attractive couple despite their solemn expressions.

They invited him into a den comfortably furnished with a leather sofa and two overstuffed armchairs. He took one of the chairs and the Malloys sat side by side on the couch.

"We were surprised to get your phone call," Jim Malloy said anxiously. "It's been a few years since we last spoke."

Donna Malloy slipped her arm through her husband's. "Is there news…" she faltered and started over. "Have you found remains?"

"Nothing like that," Sam said. "I'd just like to ask you a few questions."

"After all these years? Why?" Jim demanded. "Something must have happened. Why else would you be here?"

Sam was careful in his approach. "Has Jenna mentioned anything about Riley to you lately?"

They exchanged a glance. "We haven't seen much of Jenna since she moved out a few weeks ago," her mother said. "She's okay, isn't she? Nothing has happened to her?"

"I saw her yesterday," Sam assured them. "She seemed fine."

Jim Malloy's voice hardened suspiciously. "You talked to our daughter? Why? What aren't you telling us?"

"It seems that both Jenna and Ellie Brannon have been receiving anonymous calls from someone pretending to be Riley."

Donna Malloy gasped. "Ellie, too, this time?"

Sam lifted a brow. "Jenna has received these calls before?"

"Yes, years ago. She swore Riley was still alive and was trying to reach out to her. She even claimed to see her from time to time."

Sam remembered Jenna's bus stop story. "When was this?" he asked.

"Right after she left the hospital for the first time."

"Mr. and Mrs. Malloy, why did you take your daughter out of Penn Shepherd?"

"It's an expensive place," Jim Malloy said with a scowl. "And she didn't seem to be getting any better. If anything, she got worse."

"Did you remove her because of a patient named Hazel Lamont?"

Mrs. Malloy folded her arms around her middle and shivered as her husband leaned forward, eyes glittering like glass. "You know Hazel?"

"I've met her. She and Jenna seem extremely close."

"Abnormally close. Her doctor's words, not mine. Have you ever heard of a mental condition called folie à deux? It's where two people share a delusion. That's how the therapist described Jenna and Hazel's relationship, but I never really bought it. Hazel knew exactly what she was doing when she encouraged Jenna to believe that Riley was still alive. There was no delusion about it. She also convinced Jenna that Preacher was coming back for her."

"We think it was Hazel's way of making Jenna dependent on her," Mrs. Malloy said. "She convinced

Jenna that she was the only one who would believe her and the only one who could protect her."

"It was nothing more than a sick and twisted game to that young woman," Jim Malloy said bluntly. "She never cared about our daughter."

"So her relationship with Hazel is why you took Jenna out of the hospital?"

"We tried having her moved to a different wing. That didn't work. Hazel knew how to manipulate the staff to get what she wanted. We had no choice but to separate them permanently."

"Did you know that Jenna has moved in with Hazel?"

"We know," Jim Malloy said gruffly. "Jenna is a grown woman. There's nothing we can do legally to interfere." He paused for a moment. "You say Jenna and Ellie have both been receiving these phone calls? Why is the FBI involved?"

"The case has never been closed," Sam said. "I've never given up on finding the person or persons responsible for abducting Riley and Jenna from the Ruins that night. I follow every lead no matter how remote."

Jim Malloy looked skeptical. "I still have to believe there's something you're not telling us. You say you're here to follow a lead, but Hazel Lamont wasn't around back then. Yet all your questions have been about her. What's really going on, Agent Reece?"

Mrs. Malloy leaned forward worriedly. "Is our daughter in any danger?"

"I don't know," Sam answered candidly. "Hazel Lamont accosted Ellie Brannon in a restaurant yesterday. She made a few veiled threats about anyone who would try to keep her and Jenna apart. She mentioned the two of you. Ellie was sufficiently concerned to believe you should be warned."

Jim Malloy gave Sam another one of those hard stares. "You think we don't already know to take precautions around that woman? Why do you think we changed the locks on all our doors after Jenna moved out? Why do you think I keep a loaded gun on my nightstand?" His eyes glittered dangerously. "You know what I'm really afraid of, Agent Reece? That Hazel Lamont may somehow convince our own daughter to come into our home and murder us in our sleep."

TWILIGHT HOVERED AROUND the edges of the lake when Ellie left the studio. Sam had left a couple of texts during the interview. He was on his way back from Dallas, but would arrive a little later than he'd intended. He'd met with the Malloys and would fill her in on the conversation as soon as he saw her. He'd yet to touch base with the nurse who had worked at Penn Shepherd, but he hoped she'd get in touch just as soon as she received his message.

Ellie glanced at the time on her phone, contemplating whether or not to text him back. An hour had passed since his last message. He'd be arriving soon despite his late start. She wouldn't bother him while he was driving since she had nothing new to report.

Clutching her phone in one hand and her keys in the other, she hurried along the trail. The pistol she kept downstairs was tucked in the back of her jeans. She needed to go over and feed the peacocks, but until Sam arrived, they'd have to fend for themselves—

She halted in her tracks as she spotted someone sitting on her deck. She put the phone away and reached behind her for her weapon just as Jenna caught sight of her and rose. She came down the steps and waited for Ellie at the bottom. Her hair was tangled, her clothing askew. She looked as if she'd been running for her life.

"Ellie, thank God! I've been waiting for you for the longest time."

Ellie's hand dropped from the pistol. "I've been in the studio. What's wrong?" She caught sight of a jagged scratch down Jenna's arm and gasped. "What happened?"

Jenna grabbed her hand. "He's coming, Elle. He's coming back for us."

SAM'S RINGTONE PEALED as he exited the interstate and turned down the state highway toward Belle Pointe. He tapped his earpiece and greeted the caller.

"Special Agent Reece."

"This is Dianne Collier. You left a voice mail for me earlier?"

The name clicked and Sam said anxiously, "Yes, Ms. Collier. Thank you for calling me back. We used to speak occasionally when you worked at Penn Shepherd. This would have been about fifteen years ago. I came to the hospital on several occasions to interview a young patient named Jenna Malloy."

"I remember you well, Agent Reece. And, of course, I remember Jenna." She paused. "She's been one of the harder patients to forget. Has something happened to her? Is that why you're calling?"

Sam briefly explained the situation. After he finished, she said nothing.

"Did I lose you?" he asked.

"No, I'm still here. You say Hazel Lamont is back in Jenna's life?"

"I gather it's a recent development," Sam said. "What can you tell me about their relationship at Penn Shepherd?"

"They were roommates for a time. They grew quite close as I recall." Her tone was guarded.

"So close the doctors thought they were sharing delusions," Sam said.

"Hazel was clever and manipulative. Jenna was more subtle."

"That's an interesting observation."

"Jenna was an interesting patient. She spoke of the girl who'd gone missing as if she were still alive."

"Riley Cavanaugh."

"Yes, Riley. Jenna claimed Riley could reach out to her even in the hospital. She claimed their abductor was able to communicate with her, too. Her doctors thought at first that Jenna exhibited characteristics of dissociative identity disorder. Split personalities. To Jenna, her friend, Riley, was very much alive and forever on the run from the monster she called Preacher."

"You said *at first* her doctors thought she exhibited these characteristics."

"Jenna could be very convincing. She was also quite the actress."

"Are you saying she faked these characteristics?"

"A diagnosis of DID is rare and still somewhat controversial. It garnered Jenna a great deal of attention for a while." Another long pause. "I don't know if she was faking. What I do know is that the Preacher persona gave her an excuse to act out. I always believed it was this personality, real or not, that Hazel Lamont was most attracted to. And most susceptible to, too."

"What do you mean?"

"Everyone, including Jenna's doctors and her parents, thought that Hazel was a bad influence on Jenna. I was around those two girls more than anyone. I never saw it that way. I always believed it was the opposite, in fact."

JENNA SAT AT the kitchen table while Ellie cleaned the scratch on her arm and applied antiseptic. Neither of them said much during this time. Jenna seemed unwilling or unable to explain how she'd gotten injured or even how she'd ended up at Ellie's place. The driveway was empty. No car in sight. No sign of Hazel, either.

Ellie closed the first-aid kit and stood to wash her hands at the sink. Twilight had fallen by this time, but the horizon still glowed from the last of the sunset. Behind her, Jenna stirred.

"I left her there," she said in a voice that didn't sound like her own. "I left her in that awful place."

"You mean Riley?"

Jenna looked up through haunted eyes. "She got so sick toward the end he didn't take her away anymore. That was a relief, even though it meant he came for me more often. But at least I didn't have to lie in the dark and listen to Riley's screams."

Ellie's heart jolted. "I'm so sorry, Jenna."

She nodded vaguely. "When he came for me, I'd close my eyes and pretend to be someone else until he was done. It wasn't me he touched. It wasn't me he hurt."

Ellie came back over to the table and sat down.

Jenna went on as if Ellie's presence didn't really register. "He told us that only one of us would ever leave that awful place. Survival of the fittest, he called it. In order to be free, one would have to die by the hand of the other."

Ellie gasped as icy fingers slid down her spine. "Did you ever see his face?"

A frown flickered, as if the question confused her. "You mean Preacher? He was careful. It was always so dark and sometimes he wore a mask."

"You remember his voice, though?"

"Yes. Sometimes he whispers to me when I sleep."

Ellie closed her eyes briefly. "What happened to Riley?"

"She got weaker and weaker. She told me that I would have to be the one. She didn't have the strength. It had to be me. But I couldn't do it." Jenna grabbed Ellie's hand and squeezed. "I couldn't do it. I couldn't do it."

"Shush," Ellie soothed. "It's all over. You're safe now."

"It'll never be over," Jenna said. "Not as long as he's still out there. Not as long as he knows what I did."

Ellie shivered. "What did you do?"

"She was so hot. Her skin was on fire. I used what little water we had to try to cool her forehead with my shirt. She grabbed my hand and placed it over her nose and mouth. I knew what she was trying to do. She was trying to help me. But I couldn't do it. Not at first. Not for a long time. She just kept pleading with me to end it. She was going to die in that awful place no matter what I did. If I ended her suffering, maybe I could at least go free. She begged and begged until I finally placed my shirt over her face and pressed. After a while, she went limp but I kept the shirt to her face. I kept on pressing until her skin cooled and then I lay down beside her and waited."

Ellie could hardly speak. "What happened then?"

"He came for me one day. He blindfolded me, tied my hands behind my back and took me away. I don't know how long we drove before he stopped the car and made me get out. He untied my hands but he told me not to take off the blindfold until I counted to one hundred. I heard his car drive off, but I kept on counting. Ninety-eight, ninety-nine, one hundred. I removed the blindfold, but I still couldn't see. The sun was so bright. I had no idea where I was or even who I was by that time. But I knew what I had done."

Ellie clutched her hand. "What happened wasn't your fault. None of it was your fault."

She drew her hand away and closed her eyes. "He's coming."

Ellie sat frozen in dread. "Who?"

Jenna's voice altered subtly. Deepened. Hardened. "You know who."

Ellie rose slowly and backed away from the table. "Jenna?"

Her eyes flew open. "He's here."

Chapter Fifteen

Ellie's gaze remained riveted on Jenna. She was so taken by the look of dread in Jenna's eyes that she failed to glimpse the dark figure slipping across the deck until he—she—stood outside the door. Before Ellie had time to reach for her weapon, he kicked the door open, shattering the frame.

Someone screamed. Ellie wasn't sure if it was her or Jenna. She lunged across the kitchen floor, placing herself between Jenna and the door.

"Jenna, run!"

The command seemed to awaken her from a deep trance. She bolted from her chair and dashed for the dining room. Ellie drew her weapon, but the intruder was on her in a flash, slinging her against the counter where she crumpled like a rag doll. The gun flew from her hand and slid under the table. She scrambled toward it, but Preacher grabbed her legs and pulled her back. Then he straddled her, pinning her down as his hand closed around her throat.

Ellie tore at the knit mask while she reached frantically for her weapon. The fabric gave way, revealing the monster's face.

Cory Small swore. Jenna screamed.

Ellie fought him with every ounce of her strength, but the hand only squeezed tighter. Panic set in. Her energy waned. Still she frantically felt for the gun, her fingers finally closing around the cool metal. Shoving the pistol between them, she pulled the trigger.

He clutched his side in stunned disbelief. Ellie tried to fire off another round, but he slammed her hand against the floor again and again until she released the weapon. Then he wrapped both his hands around her throat.

A voice said from the doorway, "Federal agent! Stand down or I'll drop you on the spot."

Three shots rang out and it was over.

When Ellie was able to breathe, she scrambled across the floor where Jenna sat huddled with her knees tightly drawn to her chest.

"It's okay. It's okay. He'll never hurt you again."

Sam kicked away the weapon and checked Cory Small's pulse. Then he took out his phone and called for an ambulance and backup.

"Everyone okay here?" he asked as he hunkered beside Ellie and Jenna.

"I hope so," Ellie whispered.

Sam put his arms around both of them and held on tight.

Chapter Sixteen

Two days later...

Ellie stood on her deck at sunset, staring out at the gilded water as she reflected on everything that had happened. In between surgeries and before he'd lawyered up, Cory Small had told the authorities where to find Riley's remains, along with those of his uncle, Silas Creed. With his confession and certain evidence that had been recovered from his farm, a grim story had unfolded.

Cory had had a fascination for Riley for a long time, perhaps even years, before he'd taken her. He'd spoken to her a few times, once or twice in the presence of her friend, Jenna Malloy, who may or may not have begun to get suspicious. Cory couldn't take that chance so he backed off, covertly encouraging some of his classmates to dare the girls to go out to the Ruins. He even arranged for Tom Brannon to be lured away from the house that night, allowing the girls to slip away undetected.

Whether willingly or unwittingly, Silas Creed had become his nephew's accomplice. He had helped Cory subdue the girls and roll their bodies in plastic, using chemicals from the farm to disguise their scent from the bloodhounds. They had taken Jenna and Riley deep into the woods, to an old storm cellar that Cory had worked on for months, installing bars and padlocks.

Afterward, he killed his uncle, disposed of the body down a well and drove his truck into the river. Silas's timely disappearance had made him the main suspect, as Cory had known it would.

Ellie felt bone-deep weary from all the questions and discoveries, but strangely at peace, as if a weight had finally been lifted from her shoulders. Sam stood beside her, a calm and steady presence.

"Why didn't he just kill Jenna, too, I wonder. He took an awfully big risk letting her go."

Sam gazed out at the water. "By that time, he probably felt omnipotent. It gave him a thrill to watch Jenna out in the open and know that he could take her again at any time."

"That level of depravity doesn't manifest overnight," Ellie said. "How could his mother not have known? How could we not have known?"

"The same way serial killers fool their families and neighbors for years. Monsters aren't always quiet loners," Sam said. "But they are almost always clever and cunning. We don't know that Riley was his only victim. We'll comb the farm and woods for remains and we'll go back through the cold case files and see if we can connect him to any unsolved disappearances. But it's possible he was one and done. He might have lived forever on the crumbs of his secret if Melanie Kent hadn't turned back up, asking questions. He let her stay in Creed's shed so that he could find out what she knew. Then he must have started to worry about what you and Jenna might remember."

"Melanie went to see Jenna, too?"

Sam nodded. "Melanie's questions and Hazel Lamont's reappearance in Jenna's life created the perfect storm. Riley and Preacher started to battle inside her again. She made those anonymous phone calls to your radio show, trying to warn you. It was Jenna you saw by the lake and probably Jenna you saw in the black hat."

"The friendship bracelet, the peacock feather…all of it was Jenna. She even tried to push me over the banister at the Ruins. Preacher came back for the girl that got away, just like the Unknown Caller warned me that he would."

"After she scaled down from the roof, she probably hid out in the woods all night, trying to elude Preacher when he was there inside her all along. She came to your house to try to warn you."

Ellie shivered. "She gave me a glimpse of what she and Riley went through. He made her kill her best friend. You don't come back from something like that."

"No," Sam said grimly. "But she can get better. Riley and Preacher went away for a long time until Melanie's questions and Hazel's encouragement brought them back."

Ellie glanced at him. "What happens now? For you, I mean."

"I go back to Dallas. Back to my other cases."

"Back to chasing monsters."

His gaze narrowed as he scanned the opposite bank. "They're out there, watching from the shadows."

Ellie turned back to the water. "I'll miss seeing you every day."

He turned at that, his deep gaze taking her in. "Dallas isn't that far away. My commute in DC was almost as long. You can see as much or as little of me as you like. I'm only ever a phone call away."

"I'm counting on that." She moved closer and his arm came around her. She laid her head against his shoulder as she stared out at her beloved Echo Lake. "After all these years, it's finally over."

He pulled her close. "I prefer to think of it as just the beginning."

* * * * *

COMING NEXT MONTH FROM

HARLEQUIN

INTRIGUE

Available August 18, 2020

#1947 CONARD COUNTY: HARD PROOF

Conard County: The Next Generation • by Rachel Lee

Former soldier and newbie deputy Candela "Candy" Serrano is assigned as a liaison to Steve Hawks, the host of TV's *Ghostly Encounters*. Chasing shadows isn't Candy's idea of police work, but soon some very real killings start occuring around town...

#1948 HIS BRAND OF JUSTICE

Longview Ridge Ranch • by Delores Fossen

The only person who knows who killed Marshal Jack Slater's father is Caroline Moser. But the Texas profiler has no memory of the murder, her abduction...or Jack. Now in Jack's protective custody, Caroline must trust her ex to help her recall her past before a murderer steals their future.

#1949 PROTECTIVE ORDER

A Badge of Honor Mystery • by Rita Herron

Reese Taggart's search for her sister's stalker lands her in Whistler, NC, where she must win the trust of arson investigator Griff Maverick. But as the pair close in on the criminal, can Griff stop Reese from using herself as bait?

#1950 BURIED SECRETS

Holding the Line • by Carol Ericson

To halt construction of a casino on Yaqui land, ranger Jolene Nighthawk plants damning evidence. But she's caught by her ex, Border Patrol agent Sam Cross. As Jolene and Sam investigate a series of deaths, they find that their bodies may be the next ones hidden in Arizona sand.

#1951 LAST STAND SHERIFF

Winding Road Redemption • by Tyler Anne Snell

Soon after Remi Hudson tells Sheriff Declan Nash he's going to be a dad, Remi becomes the target of repeated attacks. Declan will do anything to keep her and their unborn baby safe, especially once he realizes the danger is related to an unsolved case involving his family.

#1952 CAUGHT IN THE CROSSFIRE

Blackhawk Security • by Nichole Severn

When Kate Monroe's deceased husband suddenly appears, the profiler can't believe her eyes. Declan Monroe has lost all of his memories, but with a killer targeting Kate, the pair will have to work together to outwit the Hunter...and find their way back to each other.

YOU CAN FIND MORE INFORMATION ON UPCOMING HARLEQUIN TITLES, FREE EXCERPTS AND MORE AT HARLEQUIN.COM.

HICNM0820

SPECIAL EXCERPT FROM

HARLEQUIN

INTRIGUE

While investigating a series of deaths in the Sonoran Desert, Border Patrol agent Sam Cross comes face-to-face with Jolene Nighthawk, the woman he once loved beyond all reason. Now, as the two join forces to get justice for the voiceless, old sparks reignite even as someone wants to make sure their reunion is cut short...

Keep reading for a sneak peek at Carol Ericson's Buried Secrets...

He grabbed his weapon and his wallet and marched out to his rental car. When did Border Patrol ever stop working? Especially when an agent didn't have anything better to do.

He pulled out of the motel parking lot and headed toward the highway. His headlights glimmered on the wet asphalt, but on either side of him, the dark desert lurked, keeping its secrets—just like a woman.

Grunting, he hit the steering wheel with the heel of his hand and cranked up the radio. Two days back, and the desert had already weaved its spell on him. He'd come to appreciate its mystical, magical aura when he lived here, but the memory had receded when he moved to San Diego. When he left Paradiso, he'd tried to put all those feelings aside—and failed.

When he saw the mile marker winking at him from the side of the road, he grabbed his cell phone and squinted at the directions. He should be seeing the entrance to an access road in about two miles. A few minutes later, he spotted the gap and turned into it, his tires kicking up sand and gravel.

His rental protested by shaking and jerking on the unpaved stretch of road. He gripped the wheel to steady it. "Hold on, baby."

HIEXP0820

A pair of headlights appeared in the distance, and he blinked. Did mirages show up at night? Who the hell would be out here?

His heart thumped against his chest. Someone up to no good.

As his car approached the vehicle—a truck by the look of it—he slowed to a crawl. The road couldn't accommodate the two of them passing each other. One of them would have to back into the sand, and a truck, probably with four-wheel drive, could do that a lot better than he could in this midsize with its four cylinders.

The truck jerked to a stop and started backing up at an angle. The driver recognized what Sam had already deduced. The truck would have to be the one to make way, but if this dude thought he'd be heading out of here free, clear and anonymous, he didn't realize he'd run headlong into a Border Patrol agent—uniformed or not.

Sam threw his car into Park and left the engine running as he scrambled from the front seat. The driver of the truck revved his engine. Did the guy think he was going to run him over? Take him out in the dead of night?

Sam flipped open his wallet to his ID and badge and rested his other hand on his weapon as he stalked up to the driver's side of the truck.

Holding his badge in front of him and rapping on the hood of the vehicle, he approached the window. "Border Patrol. What's your business out here?"

The window buzzed down, and a pair of luminous dark eyes caught him in their gaze. "Sam? Sam Cross?"

Sam gulped and his heart beat even faster than before as the beam of his flashlight played over the high cheekbones and full lips of the woman he'd loved beyond all reason.

SPECIAL EXCERPT FROM

Read on for sneak peek at Sharon Sala's
new nail-biting thriller,
Blind Faith.

One

The morning sun was hot on Tony Dawson's head, but his anger was hotter. This camping trip in Big Bend National Park was nothing but a setup—a betrayal—and by two people he had considered friends.

The drunken argument the three high school boys had last night had carried over into morning hangovers. They packed up camp in silence, and were nearing the junction that would take them back down to the Chisos Mountain Lodge where their overnight hike had begun.

Tony had nothing to say to either of them, which obviously wasn't what they'd expected, and as they neared the junction, both Randall Wells and Justin Young lengthened their strides to catch up to him.

"What are you going to do when you get back?" Randall asked.

Tony just kept walking.

Randall pushed him. "Hey! I'm talking to you!"

"Keep your damn hands off me. Not interested. Don't want to hear the sound of your lying voice. You said enough last night," Tony said.

"Are you going to keep seeing Trish? After all you found out?" Randall asked.

Tony fired back. "I had girlfriends back in California. I would assume they moved on when I left, because I did. So what if you dated Trish before I even knew her?"

"What about what Justin said?" Randall asked.

Tony stopped, then turned to face the both of them.

"You want the truth? I don't believe Justin. Why would I? You two lied about wanting to be my friend. You lied about this camping trip. It was a setup. You're both losers. Why would I believe two sore losers over my own instincts?"

Tony saw the rage spreading over Randall's face, but he wasn't expecting Randall to come at him.

Randall leaped toward him, swinging. Tony stepped to the side to dodge the blow, and when he did, the ground gave way beneath his feet. All of a sudden he was falling backward off the mountain, arms outstretched like Jesus on the cross, knowing he was going to die.

MEXPSS022

Two days later: Dallas, Texas

A Dallas traffic cop clocked the silver Mercedes at ninety-five miles per hour, and was just about to take off after it when his radar gun went dark, and then the car shot through a non-existent opening in the crazy morning traffic, before disappearing before his eyes.

"That did not just happen," he muttered, but just in case, radioed ahead for the next cop down the line to be on the lookout.

Wyrick wasn't concerned with the cop's confusion. She was already off the freeway and taking back streets to get to the office. She knew the cop had clocked her, but she had her own little system for blocking traffic radar, and she was in a bigger hurry than normal because she overslept—a rare occurrence.

Now, she just needed to get to the office before Charlie Dodge, or she'd never hear the end of it.

Finally, the office building came into view, and she sped through the last half mile without once tapping the brakes, skidded into her own parking place, and breathed a sigh of relief that Charlie's parking spot was still empty.

"That's what I'm talking about," she muttered, as she grabbed her things and got out on the run.

Within minutes of opening the office, she had coffee on, with the box of sweet rolls she'd picked up this morning plated beneath the glass dome in the coffee bar, and had both of their computers up and running.

She was going through the morning email when Charlie walked in, but she refused to look up. She knew what she looked like. She'd spent precious time this morning making sure she looked fierce, because she felt so damned wounded from the dreams.

"Bear claws under glass," she muttered. "Teenager missing in the Chisos Mountains in Big Bend. Are you interested?"

Charlie was used to Wyrick's outrageous fashion sense, and refused to be shocked by the black starbursts she'd painted around her eyes, the blood drop she'd painted at the corner of her mouth, the red leather cat suit, or the black knee-high boots she was wearing. But he was interested in the sugar crunch of bear claws, and kids who went missing.

"Yes, to both," he said, as he sauntered past. "Send me the stats on the missing kid, and get the parents in here for details."

"They're due here at 10:30."

He paused, then turned around, his eyes narrowing.

"Why do you even ask me what I want?"

"You're the boss," Wyrick said.

"I know that. I just didn't know you did," he mumbled.